Downward

Rogue Maniacs MC
Book #1

MariaLisa deMora

Editing: Hot Tree Editing

Cover: CT Cover Creations

Photography: Wander Aguiar, Photography

Model: Jamie Knight

First Published 2023

ISBN 13: 978-1-946738-8-3

DEDICATION

"One moment can change a day, one day can change a life, and one life can change the world."
~Gautama Buddha

To the folks who put up with my pained vocalizations during yoga class: Y'all are the most tolerant bunch of bendy people I know!

CONTENTS

ACKNOWLEDGMENTS

This story began like so many of mine do, with a mix of things I love and dreams that push me to dig deeper into a story. Elodie (pronounced Eh-loh-dee) was so zen with her yoga—laidback, yet with a deep side of quirkiness, I couldn't wait to pair her with a biker to help shake up her world. Then Mad Dawg came along, and it was a match made in yoga heaven.

Many thanks to Sapphire Knight for her unending support. Not only is she a fabulous friend and a talented author, but she's also hostess of an impressive book signing focused on some of my favorite tropes. Also, she loaned her hubby Jamie to me for the cover of this book. I was excited when I found the shot on Wander Aguiar's website and thrilled that It was available. Serendipity at work, right there.

I'm so pleased to be spinning tales again. It truly feeds something in my soul. Hope you enjoy this story. I had a blast writing it.

Woofully yours,
~ML

Disclaimer:
Some scenes in this book reference a real-world book signing: Motorcycles, Mobsters and Mayhem. While the event and mentioned authors are real, the scenes derived from it are not. Pure imagination here folks.

Downward Dawg

Mad Dawg is practically obsessed with his business neighbor, Elodie Forrester, the woman who owns the yoga studio next to his bike shop. He can't get her out of his mind, and hopes it's the same on her side. She does visit, mostly when loud bikes interrupt her yoga classes, but a visit is a visit, right? He's pretty sure she flirts with him, too. Pretty sure. Mostly sure.

Elodie isn't mad when a gorgeous biker opens a shop next to her yoga studio. Watching him walk from his bike to his door is her daily secret pleasure. And Mad Dawg is courteous about the quiet hours needed for the classes. Mostly. The problem is he doesn't seem to return her interest. Bummer.

Things between them start to heat up, as past miscommunications are sorted out. Can the rough and tumble biker convince the graceful and calm yogi their lives should be intertwined in a way that's lasting?

Abbreviation map:

- RMMC – Rogue Maniacs MC
- HHMC – Heartless Horde MC

Chapter One
Elodie

Elodie Forrester lay on a thin mat stretched out on the floor of her yoga studio, talking the small class through breathing and relaxing after the intermediate pose sequence they'd just finished. On her back with arms in cactus position, she angled her head to use the mirrors to check on each participant in case they needed more encouragement.

The vibration was tiny at first, nearly undetectable, but the bones of her head picked it up and Elodie closed her eyes, trying to keep hold of the relaxation she'd just been experiencing.

Within a few carefully controlled breaths, the rumble of exhaust was loud enough to be audible, and Elodie immediately decided to end the class a few minutes early. She pushed herself to an easy sitting position and talked everyone through attaining the same. After thanking them for including her in their practice, she folded her hands at heart center and tipped her head. The formal ending phrasing flowed easily from her lips, and as always, Elodie tried to infuse each word with meaning. "The light in me sees and honors the light in you. Namaste."

Class members rose, redonned exterior clothing, and exited over the next few minutes. Various groups of friends chatted and made plans for coffee or shopping, leaving Elodie standing in the warmly lit room alone. She retrieved a couple of blocks left near the wall, sanitized them, and placed them on a rack to dry. Several similarly-sanitized yoga mats hung over the railing running the length of the mirrored wall, but they wouldn't be completely dry for another half hour.

Elodie settled back onto her mat and folded her legs into easy pose. *Criss-cross applesauce.* Cupping her hands over her knees, she sought the grounding needed before she made her way next door to talk to the neighboring business owner, a man who demanded she call him Mad Dog, pronounced dawg, which in no way could be his given name. Unless his parents were even more hippy-dippy than hers.

Be hard to out-hippy the original hippies.

Since opening his shop a few months ago, Mad Dawg usually kept late hours, staying open until midnight or beyond. Thankfully however, he was closed in the mornings and on weekends, generally not unlocking his door until around two in the afternoon. This had worked well for Elodie because most of her classes were early, beginning around sunrise. Since she was the only instructor, her business was often closed before Mad Dawg's key breached the lock. But closed didn't mean she wasn't still there.

That lack of obvious overlap didn't keep her from always being on the lookout for him—after all, the man was gorgeous with a capital G. His sharp cheekbones, intelligent gaze, and an easy, self-deprecating grin were matched with a body that was broad and tall, which meant Mad Dawg was definitely a feast for the eyes. Most days found her peeking around the edge of the door to watch his well-shaped ass saunter to his door.

For the first time, bikes had come in before ten today, and Elodie wanted to know if this was the new normal, or an aberration.

I need this to be a onetime thing.

The practice of yoga required mindfulness within the poses, remembering which muscle groups to engage and which to release, and a focus on breathing ease into tension spots. If motorcycles started coming next door earlier than had been the norm, it would disrupt her entire class schedule. As it was, she worked long hours on Saturday and Sunday to provide classes for those unable to come to an early morning weekday practice.

Manifesting that this is a onetime thing. Come on, universe. Pitch me a soft one.

Elodie laughed at herself, unfolding her limbs and stretching gently as she stood. "Sure, throwing that out into the world is gonna make everything okay."

Oh, maybe he'll be wearing that soft-looking shirt.

She laughed again, and with a final glance at her reflection, made her way to the door and pulled it open. Sunshine and conversations streamed inside, the rays strong and warm, the voices low and gruff.

*****

Mad Dawg

Dominick Roberts stared at the group of bikes gathered in the front lot of the tiny shopping center where his shop occupied one narrow space. It was his dream to expand into an empty storefront just waiting on one side, but that would only happen after he'd proved to himself that he could make a living doing what he loved.

He smiled to see familiar faces mixed with new ones. Word of mouth was the best advertising, and when satisfied customers brought friends back with them, it was a good sign. When it was someone not in his own club, it was even better. He'd been blessed that the Rogue Maniacs MC members frequented his shop, but he didn't want to depend on his brothers for his livelihood.

One of the men rattled the doorknob, and when he found it locked, cupped his hands around his face, peering into the space.

Mad Dawg waved and made his way to the door, turning the deadbolt holding it closed.

"Hey, brother," he greeted the man and clasped forearms with him. "Welcome back."

"You not open yet? Shit, man, we can come back later." The man, Mad Dawg remembered his name was Alan, shoved his hands into the pockets of his jeans. "Didn't mean to bother you."

"Not a bother at all. I'm here every day, soon as I roll out of bed, but I typically don't unlock the door until I've had enough coffee to hold a coherent conversation." That pulled a laugh out of the waiting men, and Mad Dawg greeted each as they came through the door. "There's a coffee maker on the back wall, if any of you need some extra go-juice."

General murmurs of thanks and appreciation came from the group as they migrated that direction. Conveniently placed past the racks of clothing and leather that supported the lifestyle they were all involved in, a few cups of coffee was cheap incentive to bring the customers farther into the shop. He noted four different patches on jackets and vests, all smaller support or community-style riding clubs, where every party was probably a family-friendly one.

His own vest was draped over a chair in the back room. Not out here on display, because he didn't need to flaunt his association with one of the strongest clubs in the region. It was enough that he knew where he belonged, and who his brothers were. Club members from the surrounding area were frequent visitors of the store, and he definitely felt supported by their purchases, but that support was a thing that went both ways. Most club meetings he'd show up with a bag full of parts or other things, all passed along at cost, because he wasn't going to turn a buck on his brothers.

The shop was a way for him to be involved in what he loved, every single day. The construction job he'd held before hadn't allowed him that freedom, and if one of their jobs was running behind the boss could mandate overtime. Those times meant there'd been runs and meetings he couldn't attend, and it had eaten at him until he'd come up with a way to both make a living and stay true to those who held his loyalty.

Now, he couldn't imagine ever going back to asking an unsympathetic boss for a day off to attend an out-of-town weekend run. Instead, he simply propped a sign in the window saying he'd be back on Tuesday, always giving himself a Monday as a recovery day if it was a long ride. If it wasn't, he'd come in and work inventory or the other tedious paperwork that came with owning the shop.

Mad Dawg's dream plan was to have a mechanic in the back some day. As things stood now, there would be plenty of room to put in a single bay, but if he expanded into the attached space, he could keep the shop in the existing area and use the second to build up a repair and service clientele. Given it was nearly fifty miles to the closest dealership with a reliable mechanic and nothing in between there and here, he figured he'd have a healthy business just from the area's casual rider population.

But that was for tomorrow, which meant right now he needed to pay attention to the needs of his current customers. He'd just taken a step their direction when the bell over the door gave a brief jingle, the brrrrng yanking his attention to the front of the store.

Silhouetted in sunlight was a woman and at first glance he thought she might be nude. Then she took a step inside and he saw it was Elodie from next door, dressed in her neutral-colored yoga gear. The slim-fitting fabric molded to every delicious looking inch.

Feet moving on automatic towards her, his attention covertly wandered up and down her form. The mass of golden hair was pulled up in a bun that failed to control all of it, leaving tendrils to hang down in front of her ears and along her neck. Perky breasts were barely contained in a tight spaghetti strap shirt, and her nipples were on full display, hard little nubs pressed against the fabric making his mouth water. She wasn't overly endowed, but he'd never been attracted to top-heavy women. Small enough to fit his hand was a preference and Elodie matched the description exquisitely. He knew from past association that her muscled ass filled out the leggings very well, and he loved how they stretched to fit around her strong thighs and calves. She'd slipped on a pair of flip-flops to come over, and they were a weird animal print, looking out of place against the matching theme of her outfit.

Her mouth was moving, a small smile peeking out along the corners, and he realized he'd come to a stop within touching distance of the woman, but hadn't heard a word she'd said.

Clearing his throat, Mad Dawg felt foolish, but dove in with what he expected her concern was. Soon after he'd opened his shop, they'd had a couple of conversations and she'd gently indicated that peace and quiet was integral for her classes. With that in mind, he worried his earlier-than-usual customers might have disrupted things on her side of the thin wall.

"I wasn't open. Promise." He reached for her hand and halted the movement, letting his arm fall back to his side. That lack of contact burned, but it wasn't the kind of friendship they had. "They didn't know the hours."

"Okaaay." Now she was frowning around the smile still lurking on her lips. "Good to know. But I asked if you had a cup of coffee for me, too? It smelled so good when I came in, I couldn't think of anything else."

"Yes. Yup. Of course." Mad Dawg turned on his heel and bulled his way past the racks to where the men had stepped away from the coffee maker. Which was empty. "In just a couple of minutes. Yep." Working fast, he dumped the old filter in a trashcan and replaced it with new, then added water using a gallon jug left nearby for that purpose. Flipping the button to the on position, he murmured, "Coming right up."

"Thanks." There was a long pause as he turned around, surprised to find her standing close. "Mad Dawg." Her smile broke free then, beaming his direction so brightly he found himself mirroring her expression.

"Uh, Elodie, these are some customers." Mad Dawg gestured widely at the men standing close, watching the entire interaction with high interest. "Customers, this is Elodie. She owns the yoga studio next door."

"Gentlemen," she said, inclining her head slightly. "Those bikes out front sure are pretty. Nearly as pretty as Mad Dawg's."

"Thanks," one of the men rumbled, inching closer to Elodie, his gaze fixed on her scarcely covered breasts.

Mad Dawg fought back a growl of irritation. She wasn't flirting with them, and damned if he'd stand here and play witness to anyone getting the wrong idea.

He cast around for a topic, finally asking, "How'd your classes go this morning?"

The question pulled her attention back to him and Mad Dawg internally preened at the sudden disappointment on the other men's faces.

Yeah, that's right. I know things.

"Well, thanks. I felt like the sun salutation class really connected to the practice. I was pleased for them." An expression of serenity drifted across her features and Mad Dawg felt the ache in his shoulders lessen as he relaxed a little.

"Not surprised with you leading it," he complimented her. "You've got the touch when it comes to making people feel better."

Stop. Talking. Jesus Christ on a stick, you idiot.

The gurgle of the coffee maker saved him, and Mad Dawg wheeled around, giving Elodie his back. Several of the men in the store were still gathered in a semicircle around them, eyeballing him as if they'd encountered an alien lifeform.

"Did you come in solely for the coffee, or is there anything else I can help you with?" He controlled the snarl that threatened to lift his lip, but only just barely.

"Gloves."

"Balaclava."

"Jacket options for the old lady."

"Turn signal covers."

The answers came rapid-fire, and the men spread out through the store as if he'd taken a broom to their asses.

"Let me know if I can help," he called after them, plucking a clean mug from the stack and filling it three-quarters of the way. Then he added two spoonsful of sugar and topped it off with a squirt of milk he took from the dorm-sized fridge under the table. Turning back to Elodie, he held the prepared cup out to her. He was unprepared for her reaction, because instead of a "thank you," he got peals of laughter. The intoxicatingly musical sound rolled from her, and he stared, transfixed by the sight of her losing her composure. Then he looked at the mug he'd grabbed and groaned. "Just a sec." He turned to make another cup, but she stopped him with a hand on his forearm. Her palm was hot against the skin bared by his rolled-up sleeve, and he returned his gaze to her.

"I'll take this one." She fought a smile, the corners of her mouth twitching. "You got the coffee just right. How do you remember things like that? We've only shared coffee once before."

Lifting the mug to her mouth for a drink, she stared at him over the rim, dancing eyes peering from right above the words that declared "Don't be a cuntcake" with a picture of an iced cupcake covered with dick-shaped confetti.

"It was a gag gift," he blurted, unable to concentrate on anything else but her drinking from the absolutely vulgar mug. "I didn't know it migrated from the back up here."

"So, it's your personal mug. One of your favorites." She gave him a regal nod, then sipped the coffee again. "I feel honored."

"And I swear, I wasn't open. I wouldn't jack with your classes like that. I'll make a post on social media to clarify the hours so it won't happen again."

"It's not a problem for today." She finally took pity on him and lowered the mug, turning it in her hands to giggle at it again. "If your customers had been much earlier, I'd have managed, but it wouldn't have been pretty." She drained the cup and handed it back to him, cheeks bright pink. "I'll let you get back to business, Mad Daaawg."

Hellfire and fuck me. Even the way she says my name is cute.

He stood there like a stupefied bull and watched her mesmerizing ass sway back and forth on its route through the store. She paused for a moment at the door and smiled back at him, then was gone, the tiny slapping sounds from the flip-flops marking her progress as she moved out of view.

Was that a flirty smile? Saucy? What the hell? Does she like me?

He'd carried a torch for her since their first meeting. Given their forced proximity, Mad Dawg had long determined to not act on the blazing attraction he felt. Now he wasn't sure he'd managed to conceal it very well. *Plus, if she's interested, is it something I have to ignore?* It could be messy, his shop next door to her studio. *Only if things didn't work out. I'm borrowing trouble here. Likely that smile was because she thinks I'm an idiot, not because she found my flailing endearing.*

"Oh, man, you got it bad, brother." One of the few men Mad Dawg had met in this group was standing right behind him. Meant Martini had gotten the same view of Elodie's ass.

Instantly filled with irritation and the hard edge of some unfamiliar emotion, he glowered at the man. "What was it you needed?"

The man held up a hand filled with a leather jacket, patting the air with his other hand. "Down, boy. I'm already locked down. No competition for ya. Promise." He grinned. "Yeah, I found it. Already texted the old lady and she's approved."

Anger slowly subsiding to simmer just underneath the surface, Mad Dawg nodded briskly. "Let's get you rung up and on your way, then."

A small line had already formed at the register, and as he spoke with each man about their purchases, his heartbeat slowed until Mad Dawg felt relatively normal. *Thank fuck.*

Martini was the last to check out, and they tossed small talk back and forth during the transaction. As he reached for the bag Mad Dawg had placed the jacket in, Martini leaned close, cutting his eyes to one side as he whispered, "Wanted to let you know that I don't know those two guys. Think it's kinda weird that their bikes are well seasoned rides, but they don't have a vest or jacket on."

Mad Dawg looked in the indicated direction just in time to see one of the men indicate with a nod up to where the security cameras were mounted, then watched as the two men shared a glance, turned, and strode quickly out the door without making a purchase. He didn't remember even speaking directly to either of them. *Odd.* A moment later, the rumble of pipes rattled through the building and Mad Dawg gave an internal wince at the level of sound, knowing it would have totally disrupted Elodie's class if she had one now.

"I don't know them either," he said, turning his attention back to Martini. "Interesting they didn't seem to have any friends in the group of y'all. I assumed you'd all ridden in together."

"Nope. The rest of us met for breakfast at the VFW and shot the shit until we figured you'd be open. I don't think any of us knew about the afternoon thing. Sorry again about that. But I can guarantee you those two weren't with us. They tagged onto the back of the group a couple of blocks away, and just followed us in." He lifted the bag with a salute. "My old lady thanks you, and I thank you for makin' me the hero. Her old jacket started fallin' apart from being in the rain and shit. That fashion statement wasn't ever supposed to be a biker chick's jacket. I think she's learned her lesson."

"Good gear makes a difference. Dress for the slide—"

"Not the ride." Martini laughed as he walked to the front of the shop.

Mad Dawg followed Martini to the door and locked it after he walked through, lifting a hand to wave at the group of men as they rode away. He grimaced again at the noise.

"If those two think to rob this shop, they must not be real smart." He shook his head as he walked to the back room and settled in behind the computer. "Any amount of research at all, it wouldn't take a half a minute to know who I was, and the club that's got my back."

He'd have to tell his brothers the idea of having dummy cameras installed for an overt show of security was a good one. The real ones were hidden, and the system wasn't easily bypassed.

"They come knockin', we'll see who does the rockin'."

Sitting at the computer, he reopened the spreadsheet he'd been working on earlier and went back to the tedious business of inventory. Through the thin walls between the businesses, he heard the softly chiming music of Elodie's studio as a new class began. The sound was comforting, familiar, and his breathing slowed to match the pace of the music.

He liked his neighbor. More than he'd expected. Like Martini had noted, Mad Dawg had it bad.

Abandoning the spreadsheet, he opened a browser window and idly searched for the name of Elodie's yoga studio.

Clicking on the link filled the screen with soothing colors and images, out-of-focus pictures of women and men in leggings in various poses. *Leggings, as if.* There was a cycling set of graphics in the home page header, identifying various positions and giving a glimpse into the uses of each. He was surprised at how specific some were regarding the physical benefits, but then they talked about things called chakras—something he knew nothing about.

That sent him to a new browser window, and a confusing dive into a type of spirituality he'd never knew existed.

But it all fit what he knew about Elodie. She'd been calm and centered every time they'd interacted.

Confidence was a serious turn-on, and she had it in spades.

Except today. Just for a minute. She kinda acted flirty.

Then, he remembered her colored cheeks, the shy smile she'd thrown over her shoulder on the way out of the shop.

She *had* been flirting, in an understated way. Hell, even her outfit had been a statement. Previously, she'd donned a filmy overshirt before talking to him. Today?

She came over dressed like a dream come true.

He glanced back at the website, clicking on the "about" information. It had a contact form and her business address.

I wonder.

Twenty minutes later, he closed the browsers and flipped back to the spreadsheet. With the information he'd gleaned jotted on a piece of paper in his pocket, it was hard to focus on business. Mad Dawg took a moment to get plans for tonight settled in his head, then forced his brain back to work.

Later it would be time to put things into motion.

Chapter Two

Elodie

Blowing out a steady stream of air, Elodie changed position, shifting fluidly from a dynamic dragon pose to a side plank. She held the pose for ten slow breaths that got gradually shakier as time went on, then brought her body down to the mat, curling on her side in a fetal position. Monitoring her breathing, she marked the moment when her lungs no longer felt oxygen starved, and slowly fluttered her lids open.

Not two feet away was a mongrel-looking pup, eyes fixed on her in a concentrated stare.

Elodie laughed and patted the mat beside her, winding up with an armful of fluffy dog a moment later. He snuggled close, running his nose under her cheek to press as tight against her as he could manage.

"You're a good boy, aren't you, Chickie Nuggie? My boy." She ruffled the curly hair on top of Chicken Nugget's head. His blue and green eyes stayed fixed on her. Clearly the pooch had poodle and husky somewhere in his mixed lineage. "Such a good wait." He wiggled again, his whole body vibrating with joy. "You might be a Heinz 57, but you're 100 percent good boy."

She pushed to a seated position, then transitioned to her feet, avoiding placing an appendage on the dog only with difficulty. He seemed to be everywhere at once, and the level of his excitement had her looking at the clock. "Shoot and darn, I'm late feeding you. Sorry, sorry."

Once that chore was completed, Elodie showered and pulled on her favorite flannel pajamas, then stood waiting at the back door as her dog took care of business. Wet hair trailed uncomfortably along her neck, and she grimaced as Chicken ran back through the door. Elodie grabbed a fresh towel from the clean bin next to the dryer, and barely beat the dog to the couch. She bundled her hair into the towel, twisting it into a turban.

"Okay, what shall we watch tonight?"

Together they picked out a movie, a new one featuring a story by one of her favorite authors, D.M. Earl. Smiling, Elodie settled in to watch the show, barely begun when she first heard the now-familiar rumble of a motorcycle. Way out here in her out-of-the-way, cul-de-sac type neighborhood, the sound was an extremely unlikely occurrence. Frowning slightly, Elodie clambered to her feet, pausing the movie as she tossed the blanket in a drape over the back of the couch.

Chicken arrived before her at the front door, dancing on his lively paws, but Elodie had her hand on the knob before the echoes of the motorcycle had died away. "Back, Chickie Nuggie. Sit, please."

She swung the door wide to see Mad Dawg outside, still sitting astride his huge, black motorcycle. Instead of the soft-looking T-shirts he wore around the shop, he was zipped into a leather jacket that gave him an air of danger. Elodie felt a tiny frisson of fear chatter down her spine, because at first glance he didn't appear to be her eager-to-please business neighbor. No, this man was a biker, through and through. That feeling was immediately followed by the flush of interest and excitement that'd had her watching him every chance she got. *I've known him for months, and he's never given me any reason not to trust him.*

Still, biker equaled … *outlaw.* The word flashed through her mind and Elodie mentally shook her head, dismissing the idea. The man owned a small business storefront in a strip mall, for goodness' sakes. The two things didn't compute. *My gut says he's one of the good ones.* The fear died away, leaving a thrill in its place. *He's here.* She didn't know why, but the fact he'd sought her out made her smile.

"Hi," she called in welcome, lifting a hand. Chicken scooted close enough his sweeping tail hugged the back of her legs, a low, never-ending growl vibrating through him. "Imagine meeting you here. Is something wrong?"

If Mad Dawg had looked large in his store, and big sitting on the bike, when he swung his leg off and stood upright clad in black leather, he was huge as a mountain, with a face as frozen as the largest slab of granite.

Yeah, something was definitely wrong. He always had a smile for her.

"Nothing's wrong," he told her, and she immediately wished for the ability to hear lies, because... well, right now he was being a lying liar MacLiarson.

She made a soft scoffing sound. "Okay, well. That's good. Glad to hear it. So, how did you know where I live?" While they'd shared several conversations over the months, none of them had been an exchange of personal information. "Pretty sure I'd remember telling you that."

The tension in his face relaxed slightly at her joking tone. "You listed your home address as the contact for your website."

He'd said the words as if they'd make sense, and she cocked her head to the side in case that'd make it better. *Nope. Still wonky.*

"My website. You got my address from my website? What? Why? And why are you here? If nothing's wrong?

Not that I mind you being here." She gestured at the bike vaguely. "But don't you have biker things to do?" *In my favorite books, there are always biker things to do.* She was still a bit confused at his casual statement about her website. *Mental note to check my private info isn't public.* It wouldn't do to have studio members showing up at her home. *Or stalkers, unless it's cute biker ones.*

"Nah, church is tomorrow night." He shrugged as he walked towards her, the bottom edge of his jacket skimming right on top of his narrow hips, which sat above his tree trunk thighs, ready for her to climb.

Gah. Stop looking at him like that.

"Church?" Since he didn't look like he'd be stopping his forward momentum anytime soon, she stepped graciously to the side and with a grin and a sweep of her hand, gestured towards the interior of the house. Her invitation was belated, and heavily laced with sarcasm when she told him, "Please, come on in."

"Thanks." His head swiveled from side to side, apparently taking in everything. "A meeting. Club meeting."

"I'm sorry, what?" Elodie realized she was still in the open door and slowly closed it, letting the catch slip into place silently. Chicken was still plastered to the back of her calves, but he'd finally stopped making noise. "Oh, church is a meeting. A biker kind of meeting. I think I knew that. Sorry, I'm still stuck on why you're here if nothing's wrong at the shop."

He glanced at her, and as always, the weight of his gaze was like a physical touch. Having his full focus was heady, and Elodie fought to hide her pleasure. "Nothing's wrong, exactly. But there were a couple of men in my store today I didn't know, and it looked like they were casing the place. Nothing for you to worry about, but I thought you should know." His face hardened. "Being a good neighbor, you know?"

"Oh, pressing news. Yes. But I'm thinking you could have told me this tomorrow when you opened up." She glanced at the TV, screen still frozen where she'd paused it.

"I could have. But I wanted to see you." He said this like it made sense, and really it should. The way his eyes stayed fixed on her lent his words gravity, and she remembered their flirty exchange from earlier today.

Warning first, then seeing me could be a bonus side quest, maybe? Could be he lives nearby, even. It wasn't out of the realm of possibility that he'd wanted to give her the message tonight, knowing she'd be at the shop early, in the dark and alone. The thought of him caring was kind of endearing, honestly.

There is one more possibility. She might have read things wrong with him. *Maybe* we *weren't flirting, just me.*

"Oh. If it's about today and me interrupting your business, I can apologize."

"None needed." He shifted on his feet as he stayed facing her, hands shoved deep into his jacket pockets. "I enjoyed every bit of your company. Always do. Thing is, I rarely get a chance to really talk to you. Most of what we do is just hello, goodbye, you know?" His shoulders reached up towards his ears in a shrug that somehow looked adorably shy. The movement made her want to reassure him he hadn't overstepped. "So, I kinda thought I'd make the opportunity."

Elodie stared at him for a moment, running their various interactions through her mind. She let her awareness focus back on how he made her feel and the vibes he put off. With a sense of happiness, she realized that every time she was around him, she felt lighter for the encounter. *We vibe.* They resonated in a good way. There was also that frisson of lust, and the way her emotions had moved straight from "he's attractive" to "boy, I bet he'd be good in the sack."

She smiled at him, letting her pleasure show in her expression, decision made. *He's not a threat to me.*

"Chicken and I were watching a fluff romance and eating bad-for-us snacks." She gestured to the couch. "I can share the blanket, but you'll have to find your own stuff to snack on. It's enough of a trial to have to share with the doggo." She bent at the waist and unwound the towel from her hair, ruffling through the strands with her fingers for a moment before standing back upright. Flinging her still-damp locks over her shoulder, she shrugged at him. "Right, Chicken?"

With the repetition of his name, Chicken came around her and planted himself midway between the two of them. He plopped his ass to the ground, then twisted around to lick where his balls used to be. Elodie smiled wider.

"Oh, Chickie likes you. That move means he's comfortable."

"You named your dog Chicken? Seems counterintuitive. Dogs eat chicken." Mad Dawg shrugged his jacket off, and sure enough, hidden underneath was another one of those super-soft-looking shirts that molded to his muscles, emphasizing every lickable nook and crevice of his hard frame. He looked around and headed towards the front of the house. "One of my brothers has a dog named Dog, though, so it's more inventive than that at least." Jacket hung on a hook near the door, Mad Dawg turned and walked back to her. "Point me to the kitchen?"

"Through there." She tipped her head the direction and stayed where she was to watch him walk away.

"You're lookin' at my ass, aren't you?" His voice carried amusement, and he glanced over his shoulder, eyes twinkling with humor as he caught her in mid ogle.

"You do it too," she defended, feeling a blush climb up from her chest.

"Well, you've got a mighty fine ass." He disappeared and she heard the clink as the fridge opened. A pause, then another clink as the door closed. He reappeared with a beer in hand, and she realized she was still standing in the exact same spot.

"So do you," she blurted before clapping a hand over her mouth. Rolling her eyes, she sprinted to the couch and contemplated vaulting over the back, but had a flash image of headwounds or broken bones, so instead slipped into place over the arm, bouncing on the springs as she gathered the blanket to cover her legs. Mad Dawg's presence in her space had her flustered, but any sense of unease had faded as they'd bantered back and forth. Through the months she'd come to know him, each interaction between them had fleshed out an initial impression of a good man, and right now she felt strongly any danger inside him would never be aimed at her. His protective instincts with her earlier today hadn't escaped her attention, and knowing he'd felt some kind of way about those customers looking at her gave her courage.

"You promised to share that," he reminded her, taking a position on the couch not too far away. His tone turned amused when he asked, "You're not a scammer, are you? I'd hate to think I was friends with someone like that."

"No. Of course I'm not. I'm not like that. I do yoga. People like me aren't scammers. The nerve!" She playfully flipped a corner of the blanket his direction. "There."

He latched onto it and gave a tug, grinning as it rocked her closer to him. "I'm thinkin' sharin' means more than two paltry inches."

"Okay." She released her hold with a laugh. "You're right. Plus, I always keep my promises."

"Always?" His question came from beside her ear, and Elodie's breath hitched as he leaned close and spread the blanket over them both, reaching across to tuck it in on her other side. The intimate action made her skin buzz with anticipation of a real touch. *He's right here, just where I imagined him so many times.* "That's good to know. So, tell me, where does the dog named Chicken sit?"

"He's under the blanket already." She pulled in a slow, calming breath and pulled down an edge to show him. "He's sneaky."

"I'll say." Mad Dawg chuckled, the sound resonating within her chest. Every single thing this man did or said made her more aware of her attraction to him. "With a name like that, it's gotta have a story to go along with it, right? You gotta tell me. How'd Chicken get his name?"

"Well, his full name is Chicken Winston Nugget, after the first thing he stole from me *and* the first book he chewed up. You can guess the first, but the second was a first edition biography of Winston Churchill. At the time I thought of calling him Churches, as in Chicken Churches Nugget, but not everybody knows that's a chicken place. And the nuggets were a big deal. After waiting a week for his stray hold to expire, I'd just picked him up from the shelter and the first thing we did was get him a pup-latte and fries. The nuggies were supposed to be for me. Well, by the time we got to the end of the drive-thru, he'd plowed through the whipped cream, taters, and then moved on to the good stuff." She fondled his ears gently, ruffling the bouncy, curly topknot. "I figure he must have been food deprived at one point, so I couldn't be mad at him." Looking up at Mad Dawg, she felt her features soften in response to the tender expression on his face. "Anyway, Chicken Nugget seemed like a good name. Then he ate Winston, so I added that."

"You're a complicated woman, Elodie. Layers and layers. Lots to get to know." He reached out and traced a fingertip around the shell of her ear. "I don't hate that about you."

"Movie," she exclaimed, wanting to both pull away and press into his touch at the same time. More exciting than she'd anticipated, the grazing caress stole her breath, opening her mind to so many available options with him. *You're acting like a dork. It's just an ear, woman, which is not a normal erogenous zone on you. Stop it now.* "Yeah. So, ah, we were going to watch a movie." Moving too quickly, the remote flew from her hand aiming directly at his face. He smoothly caught it with his other hand, beer tucked between his thighs. "I'm so sorry." Smiling nervously, she plucked at the edge of the blanket. "Person holding the remote gets to drive. Means you've got to pick something." The TV had moved to the screensaver slideshow, having been paused too long.

"You said you and Chicken were already knee deep into a romance, right?" He flipped to recently viewed and her stomach lurched. All he'd find there was romance, romance, and more romance. Each time one of her favorite authors had a new movie come out, she'd be on it like a shot. With the new streaming services, that meant there was not a single explosion to be seen on her queue of shows and movies. Would it make him rethink his visit, knowing she was a hopeless romantic? *Hope not.* "This one? Looks likely. Lots of mush. Let's finish it. You can catch me up on anything important I missed."

"You want me to talk during a movie? Other than sharing I've actually met the person who wrote this story? It was at a Texas author event, one of my favorites. D.M. Earl was absolutely lovely to talk to. She felt real and honest in a shirt-off-her-back kind of way. I got really good vibes from her. Best friend vibes. You know? So then, chatting with her made me appreciate D.M.'s books even more. When I found out about the movie I was so excited for her. She's an indie author, so a movie deal? Unheard of and huge! So, okay, the brief on this movie is it's about Tink, president of the Devil's Handmaidens, a female motorcycle club. She's out to rid the world of human trafficking. She's awesome! But, me talk during the movie? Nevah!" Elodie mugged for him, rolling her eyes wildly. "Hand over your man card, immediately."

"Not a chance. Man card stays in the wallet. Which means we'll watch silently, and I guess I'll just be in suspense the whole time. Instead of a romance, it'll be an art flick for me, where the ending doesn't make sense. I'm good either way." He stared intently at the TV as he tugged the blanket a tiny bit. She held tight with both hands, keeping it in place. Lips curling into a smile, he told her, "Just makin' sure you didn't have more than your share."

She studied his profile. Full lips, noble brow, nose that had been broken at least once. But still, every vibe he gave off said he was a good man. She trusted her intuition. Always had. After all, it had been seldom wrong.

Don't be wrong this time. This is me manifesting hope. Gimme, universe. Gimme.

Taking a leap of faith, Elodie leaned closer, squishing Chicken between them and lightly rested her cheek against his shoulder. "I'm a good sharer. Here's a little more blanket just for you."

Mad Dawg let out a huge breath in a whoosh, like he'd been rewarded with something he'd wanted for a long time.

I got it right.

Chapter Three
Mad Dawg

Standing at the back wall of the shop, he stared at the coffee maker as if that would make it brew quicker.

"I need one of those steal-a-cup things. Whatever they are." He yawned. Waiting for the final gurgle was always the hardest, but today it was especially painful.

There hadn't been much rest to be had for him. By the time Elodie had gone to sleep next to him on the couch, gradually slouching down until her head was in his lap and her dog curled up at his hip, he'd been well and truly ensnared. The thought of moving and waking her had been painful to contemplate, so he'd spent several hours longer than he should have just watching her in the wavering light of the TV. She was a quiet sleeper, stillness infusing every muscle, as if her body was all in on the idea of recharging, and conserved everything during the shutdown.

The late hour had finally forced his hand and he'd slipped out from underneath her by bare inches at a time, pausing each instant she so much as snuffled. Finally free, with the blanket tucked securely around her and the dog, he'd dared to bend and press a gentle kiss against her cheek. That had pulled a contented sound from her, something that made his already stiff dick ache.

Forcing himself to the door, he'd gathered his jacket and walked through, ensuring it locked after him.

He'd kept the bike's rumble as quiet as he could, rolling slow and easy away from her house with a muted roar. Once on the road, he'd opened the engine up, taking himself home where he'd managed to catch a couple hours of restless sleep before the unaccustomed alarm pulled him from slumber.

Which brought him to here and now, standing in the shop at the ass-crack of dawn without even a single cup of coffee running through his veins. Another yawn snuck up on him, jaw cracking with the force. The coffee maker made its final burbling sounds, and he grabbed a cup, sorely tempted to just upend the carafe into his mouth.

Car sounds from the alley outside the back door had him moving that way and he stepped out just as Elodie stood beside her car. The shock on her face was comical, mouth opening and closing a few times before she snapped it tight.

"Mad Dawg?"

"Yes, ma'am." He walked to her side and leaned in, remembering at the last moment he was the only one of them who remembered the cheek kiss from the night before. He straightened and offered her a sloppy salute as he said, "Just me, all bright-eyed and bushy tailed." His statement might have been more believable if he hadn't yawned in the middle. "Or at least here."

"Why? You don't open for hours." Stepping to the back door, she reached inside to pull out a pile of pillows. "Shouldn't you still be sleeping?"

"Just keeping an eye on things. I didn't like the idea of you being back here alone." He gestured to the alleyway extending on either side of their vehicles. "In the dark."

"It's always dark when I get here. That's the important period right before sunrise, which is when I open for the practitioners of sunrise salutations. Five days a week. By myself." Her reminder to him had a little heat in it, a reminder that she'd never needed him to defend her against the haunts before. "Today's no different. I'd appreciate your efforts except you don't look like you got a wink of sleep."

"I managed a couple hours." He shook his head. Defending his habits wasn't why he was here. "Until I know for sure those guys aren't a threat, I thought I'd provide an extra buffer. You know. Just in case."

"Just in case." She closed the back door of her car with one hip, then leaned against the vehicle. "'In case' sounds like you know an awful lot more than you said."

"No, not really. Like I mentioned, there's a meeting tonight where I might find out more. I hope to, but it's hard to say." He'd forwarded the surveillance video of the two men to the club's technical specialist, and it was being run through facial recognition software right now. What was discovered would depend on who the men were, and what their affiliations might be. *Given everything I saw, there's absolutely no way they're not members somewhere.* "Humor me?"

"Humor you." The smile he'd come to look forward to teased along the edges of her mouth. "And let you run yourself ragged escorting me the eight feet from my car to the back door of my studio?"

"Yeah. I don't mind escorting you. It's no hardship. Trust me."

"I really enjoyed our movie night. And I slept like a baby." The abrupt change of conversation left him floundering for a moment. She continued, "You smell like fresh coffee. I'm not into chemical enhancements, except for caffeine. So, you gonna gift a needy girl with a cup'o java?"

In response, he offered her his elbow and silently held his breath until she tucked her small hand into the crook. He could feel the heat of her skin through the folds of his shirt sleeves. The touch of her fingers curling around his arm was satisfying something inside him, and his chest puffed up a little. His assistance wasn't needed in any way, but the gracious acceptance gratified his pride. He heard a quiet hum from her, then she gave a tiny jump and he realized she'd skipped to get into step with him.

He couldn't have stopped the smile that burst forth if he'd tried.

No way I'd want to shut any part of this down.

"You take your coffee the same way if it's the first cup of the day?" Swinging the door to his shop open, he let her step through ahead of him. "I'm a full strength person for that initial cup."

"I don't know another way to enjoy my coffee. Sugar and cream for me, all the way." She gifted him with a tiny smile as she looked around his still-dark shop. "It's nice and quiet in here. Do you usually have music playing?"

"Nah. I just listen in to whatever you're playing for the day." His admission was met by what he took as a satisfied sigh. "I like the tunes you play."

"So do I." She stopped next to him, her slim hip a breath away from touching his denim-clad one. "I'm pleased to find out the enjoyment doesn't stop with the walls between us."

Doctored mug in hand, he turned to her and held it out silently. She took it just as quietly. So, one way too-quick cup of coffee later, he ushered her from his door to the one of her studio, standing silent guard with an armful of pillows while she unlocked the deadbolt and disarmed the alarm.

She turned and paused. "I'll see you around, Mad Dawg." Elodie smiled at him, full on, and the brilliance of it was blinding.

She's like the sun, the brightest thing I've ever seen.

***

Elodie

After a full week of the early morning greetings, she'd stopped being surprised by Mad Dawg's appearance next to her car window. It seemed his vaunted meeting had turned up nothing useful, so his sleep continued to be interrupted by what she considered a wildly misplaced sense of chivalry.

Elodie climbed out of the car as she beamed up at him, an expression that never failed to gain a return smile. Through their brief and somewhat sleepy conversations, she'd come to realize he liked it a lot when she smiled.

Making her way to the door with hands full of keys and infusion scents, she nodded. "Mornin' Mad Dawg."

"Morning Elodie. How was your night?" As had become their routine, he propped the door open with an elbow, letting her enter before him.

"I slept well, thank you." Once she had her hands free and the alarm disarmed, he passed over today's meticulously made mug of coffee. She was amused to find the cup was the same "cuntcake" one that she'd found hilarious before. He looked on as she took the first sip.

"Coffee okay?" This was another tiny bit of routine interchange, because he always checked her read on the suitability of the caffeinated offering. "It's a new brand. I like it. Tastes smooth."

"It's perfection. Thank you so much." She paused, then asked, "So, what's on your agenda for the day?" Elodie turned on the heated floors in the studio, then rolled the stand with blocks to one side of the front door. "Big day ahead, getting ready for the weekend? I don't do sunrise classes Saturday and Sunday, which means you can sleep in if you want."

"I'm headed down state for a couple of days. Looking for more info, if it's available. I'd like to put a pin in what it meant by these guys coming around." The frown on his face was focused and heavy, his mood no longer seeming susceptible to her lighthearted conversation starter. "You're covered, though. Promise. I've got someone who'll come in the mornings when I can't be here."

"Mad Dawg." She offered him another smile. "I'm fine alone, promise. I've opened the studio early for a long time, and never had issues. I told you I think I'm here way too early for the bad guys to even be rolling out of bed." Coming closer to him, she rested a hand against his bicep. "I'll be fine."

"I'd rather not take the chance." His big hand covered hers, fingers curling around and giving her a squeeze. Her heart skipped a beat, belly quivering as it had each time he'd done something affectionate. "Humor me, yeah?"

"Humor you. That's what you've been saying for days." She shrugged lightly. "Whatever floats your boat, Dawg." She aimed for entertaining, and it seemed this hit the mark, because he finally smiled at her, albeit briefly. "That's your new name, I think. Dawg. Easier than linking two syllables together. That's just so much effort." She wiped the back of one limp wrist across her forehead, pulling away from his grip to prop it on her hip. "I simply cannot be bothered anymore."

"Well, if sayin' my name is too much, then I guess I can accept a nickname." Rolling his eyes, he chuckled. "Maybe I'll start calling you Ella, or just El, since two syllables are a chore."

"Lemme think. Meh, I don't hate Ella." Honestly, it was loads better than the Lo-Lo her mother had called her throughout childhood, but she wouldn't be offering him the other option. *He gave me a nickname back! That has to mean he likes me, right, universe?* She fought a smile, loving their playful exchange. Angling her head regally, she proclaimed, "I accept your token of affection."

"Token of affection?" He lifted his mug and finished off his coffee. Lowering it, he stared at her intently, then broke into a smile. "Is that what Dawg is, then?"

"Of course," she said brightly. "If I didn't like you, I wouldn't pick on you."

"Good to know your love language is filled with pranks and irritation."

"Oh no." She pressed one hand against her chest and pretended to be offended. "You've got me figured out."

"Jesus," he muttered, looking down as his smile widened. "You're something else, Ella."

"So are you, Dawg." She handed him her empty mug, flicking the cupcake with one finger. "This is officially my favorite mug you have. Just so you know."

"Figures." He made his way to the door and paused, hand on the knob. "Lock this behind me, yeah? And don't forget, I'll see you in a few days. My guy should be waiting just outside tomorrow morning. Don't tell him he's not needed, because if he bails on the assignment, I'm gonna be pissed. Royally." His face hardened. "To be clear, he'll be the one in hot water, not you. So don't do it to him, yeah?"

"Okay. I don't entirely understand the dynamic, but I promise not to release him from his duty. I'll leave that for you to do once you get back." She shook her head. "As long as you realize it's really not needed, you goof."

"I don't know any such thing. The info is still mixed on what's happening, and until I get a crystal-clear idea, I'm going to err on the side of caution where you're involved."

"But not when it touches you?" Elodie frowned, not liking the obvious delineation he held between them. "Buddy, that doesn't work for me. Not at all."

"Ella, I'll be as safe as I can be. That's the promise I can offer you." He adjusted the cups to dangle from one finger and lifted his other hand to his chest. Fingers spread over his heart, he stared at her intently. "Safe as I can."

"I'll take it, since that's all you can offer, Dawg. See you when you're back."

"Yes, you will." With that second promise, the door was closing behind him just as the front door chimed softly, letting her know her first class attendees were arriving.

Elodie turned with a smile on her face, easily swinging into instructor mode.

Chapter Four
Mad Dawg

He stared across the bar at Denver, who'd taken on the job of serving up drinks at this members-only church. Denver held his gaze, even as his hands busily worked to pull beers from the cooler to set on the bar top. Members were crowded into the room, but as he'd talked about Ella and his concerns, a circle of space had appeared around where Mad Dawg stood.

"What do you mean they're after me?" He repeated what he'd just heard slowly, because Denver's statement didn't make sense. "That's not something that should be. Not personal-like. Hell, other than seeing them in my shop the one time, I never put eyes on them. Fuck, man, I haven't done shit to them."

According to Denver's information, the threat had been identified as the Heartless Horde MC. They were a club who'd recently opened a chapter two towns down the highway from where Mad Dawg had his shop. His hometown was historically neutral territory, so the Rogue Maniacs hadn't offered argument to the HHMC's occupation of a different town. As for them targeting him personally? As SAA of the nomad chapter of the Maniacs, he was an officer, sure, but not a high ranking one. *I sure don't have much pull. Not like the other officers.*

"That's just what the word is. Those fucking condoms don't like having opposing representation so close to their new charter. According to them, that makes you a threat. Personal like." The patch illustration for the HHMC was a French bulldog, and one of the RMMC had mentioned that the word Frenchie used to be synonymous with condom, and thus their nickname was born. Denver shoved a bottle towards him with a shrug. "I know it's fucked up, since your shop predates their organizational location decision, but it is what it is."

Denver was the information officer for their mother chapter, where church was being held tonight. If anyone had good info, it would be him, which was why Mad Dawg had reached out as soon as things felt off. It hadn't taken Denver long to identify the men, but the track of communication between clubs was narrow and slow. Mad Dawg would have liked to have the knowledge before now. It might have changed who he'd asked to watch over Ella.

Shaking his head, he asked, "Why would they think knocking me down won't be seen as a hit against the club itself? Maniacs stand strong, you know? The only thing that would make sense was if they didn't expect any blowback. I just don't think that's reality. Not by a long shot. I might not be a big player, but the club backs our own." He lifted the bottle and took a strong pull. His bag was already upstairs, holding his place on a cot, which gave peace of mind that he wouldn't have to worry about blowing high if he got pulled over. No riding under the influence for him. *Not tonight. Not ever.* So, tonight was the perfect time for a drink or three with his brothers.

"They'd reap blowback to the extreme, and you fuckin' know it" came from next to him, and Mad Dawg turned to find Rocker at his shoulder. The man was a solid club member, and one of Mad Dawg's favorites among the brothers. "They dick around with you, might as well script their own called shots. We'd be there in a fuckin' heartbeat. On 'em like a fuckin' heart attack. Like mud on a hen, brother. Extreme blowback."

"I still don't understand why me?" Mad Dawg finished his beer and exchanged the empty for a full one Denver already had waiting. "I'm not central to the club. I'm on the edges of everything, sure, but the edge isn't in the middle. There's a reason I wear a nomad patch."

"Word is you're on the table for an upgrade." Rocker grinned at him. "Do good work and you get more work; you know how it is."

"Fuck, man, I don't want more. I'm unreasonably happy with where I am. Beyond happy."

"Aw, that's cute how you think you got a say in shit. Mad Dawg, you know how this goes." Denver rolled his eyes as he took a drink of his own beer, then tipped it towards Mad Dawg in a salute. "Your wants and needs don't matter."

"Brotherhood and club, in that order. Followed by members as a distant third." He agreed wholeheartedly with the statement. That profound respect was something he tried to live every day. "I know, but still. Shit, man."

"Couldn't happen to a better man." Rocker thudded a fist against Mad Dawg's shoulder. "Time for church, brother. Let's find seats before we're left standing along the wall like dillweeds."

The gavel in the hand of Tinder, their East Coast regional president, thudded hard against the top of a broad scarred table and Mad Dawg joined the slow scramble to find chairs. By the time the gavel had landed a third time, every man was either seated or standing quietly along the edges of the room.

Business proceeded as normal, with chapter petitions for changes or expansions handled by the regional officers. It helped to have everything done in open church, because no one chapter could be favored, or it'd be called out by all the others. For an officer, every church was mandatory, and for members it was every other, allowing for emergencies before they'd catch a fine. That meant every member who could be present, would be, holding their excused absence in abeyance.

Tinder looked around the room, his sharp gaze glancing across Mad Dawg before returning and coming to a halt. He groaned internally, knowing he was about to be singled out. "More business. Our brother Mad Dawg has brought a potential threat to our attention. As documented by our brother Denver, the HHMC has internally issued a direct threat against Mad Dawg. Standing as our current SAA for the Nomad Charter, that's going to be a serious offense from that raggedy group."

Mad Dawg waited, knowing better than to interrupt Tinder, even if it seemed the man was done speaking. A couple of beats later, his reticence was rewarded, because his president continued, "However, seein' as Wallace wants to retire to the happy land of coupledom and fatherhood, I propose a slight change in status."

Slight change my ass.

Tinder shot him a glower cut through generously with twinkling amusement in his eyes. Wallace was the current nomad chapter president and had moved around the room so he was posted up at Tinder's shoulder. The man nodded and his gaze locked on Mad Dawg, too.

Dammit, it's an ambush.

"Wallace, you got something to say to the club?" Tinder turned slightly to look up at the older man. "Now's your time, my man."

"Yeah, I do. I'd like to go inactive and can't do that while I hold an officer patch. Wouldn't be right to put the club in that kind of position, so I've put forward a couple of recommendations to leadership." Wallace folded his arms across his chest, looking about as dangerous as an overstuffed teddy bear. It was mostly a true image. Wonderful Wallace had been the man's nickname for a long time, because there wasn't a truer member in the club. But as Tinder had alluded to, he'd found an old lady who'd stuck, and was right now pregnant with their second child. With two babies in diapers in his near future, everyone knew he'd have to step back sooner or later.

Guess it's sooner.

Tinder picked up the thread, a rare grin looking awkward on his face. He was much better versed in the universal scowl than he was smiling. "We've a nomination for Mad Dawg to step up and accept the nomad president role. I think it's well timed, because being SAA is good, but he'll have more authority as a chapter president." The scowl returned, settling into the creases formed around its steady presence. "I'd like to see those assholes come at him now. All in favor of allowing Wallace to go inactive in good standing, locking up his vest and colors in the club cabinet and promoting

Mad Dawg to chapter president say aye, and any naysayers can go get fucked. This one isn't up for debate."

A rousing round of "ayes" flooded the air and hands slapped Mad Dawg's back and shoulders. Just as easy as that, his promotion within the club and chapter was a done deal, without his input or acceptance. It wasn't that he wouldn't do the job, but it would have been nice to be asked.

"Hey, Mad Dawg, you okay with this?" As if he'd read his mind, Rocker shouted over the loud crowd of well-wishers.

"Honored," he answered in the only way he could. And he realized it was the truth.

***

Elodie

She gave the unfamiliar man waiting for her a nod as she slipped from her car. He was the third one in the few days that Mad Dawg had been missing. *Not missing. Just not here. Shape up the thoughts and stop wallowing, woman. Man's got a right to have a life, you know.* Balancing the keys and a stainless steel mug of coffee in her hands, Elodie tossed a "Hello," over her shoulder.

"Mad Dawg told you I'd be here, right?" His gruff voice came from directly behind her and a hand appeared over her shoulder, taking the coffee from her fingers.

She flinched away from him, shaking hands spearing the key at the lock. "Yes," she offered as she finally got the door unlocked. None of the other men had given her the heebie-jeebies. *Get your shit together.* Scurrying inside, she dropped the keys on the counter and turned back to see him fiddling with her alarm, closing the door that covered the small keypad. "What are you doing?"

"Makin' sure you didn't call the cops." He turned back to her and lifted the coffee, drinking it down. "Thanks for the joe." He dropped the mug to the floor with a clatter as he whirled on his heels. The door slammed shut behind him just as the alarm started to beep, letting her know she had fifteen seconds to disarm it.

A bike roared to life behind the store as she speed-walked to the alarm panel and keyed in the number sequence to silence the beeping.

"Not sure why he didn't just do that. The alarm code is right there."

She turned back to the studio and sighed. Floor heaters, mats, blocks, and bolsters were waiting to be attended to.

"And all without my cup of coffee. What a jerk. At least the other two men were nicer."

Wish Dawg was back. He'd doctor me a cup just right. Putting that out there, universe. I'd like Dawg to doctor me.

Elodie smiled as she stripped off her jacket, beginning her morning routine.

***

Mad Dawg

Standing at the kitchen counter, he stared around at his furniture with a sigh. His place wasn't personalized, being barely filled with rented furniture that a brother's old lady had picked out. Nothing had been hung on the walls to soften things, and there were no blankets thrown over the back of a chair to indicate anyone spent time here. It was entirely at odds with Elodie's place, which was welcoming and warm.

Like someone actually likes to live there.

"Yeah, I'm so not bringing her here." She'd unfortunately get the right idea from seeing his home. He definitely wasn't domestic; had never developed the gene that caused some men to learn how to make things match. He could grill a mean steak, but someone like Elodie wouldn't be interested in red meat for every meal.

He could either ensure every date they had ended at her house, or he could tap another old lady for some help.

Or, newsflash, I could ask Elodie for that help instead.

He shook his head at the random thought. "She's not going to want to help me pick out curtains." He glared at the window, sporting only a set of mini-blinds. "And she sure won't want to teach me to cook."

With previous relationships, if they could be called that, he hadn't agonized over his inability to cook even a casserole. Those women had been tucked in between deployments. Space fillers, kind of like the furniture here. This thing with Elodie was different, though. Way different. He'd never spent months just getting to know a woman, and now realized everything before her only been hookups, nothing that felt real. He wanted Elodie to look at him with interest, not pity. "Gotta admit, it is kinda pitiful that you can even fuck up scrambled eggs, though."

It was just once.

Arguing with himself wasn't getting him any closer to making the call he'd wanted to since he'd finally arrived back home. He'd checked in with the prospect assigned to her detail, and found nothing had happened, which was good news, as well as exactly what he wanted to hear. Then the asshole had to mention how nice she looked in her yoga gear, and for the benefit of the prospect's health it was a damn good thing they'd been on the phone instead of in person. As it was, that prospect would now be on clubhouse latrine duty for the next month, and the man had shown enough smarts not to argue about it. *Just "yes patchholder" coming from him was the right answer.*

Mad Dawg flexed his muscles.

President for a couple of days and it's already making me mad with power.

He laughed at himself.

"So, if I can't wow her with my decorating and culinary skills, maybe a little road trip would be fun."

Decision made, he dialed her number, puzzled when her voicemail kicked in.

"Hey, Ella, it's Dawg. I wondered if you were free for dinner tonight. Let me know. You got my number." The line clicked as he hit the disconnect button and he studied the screen. It was still connected, and when he put the phone to his ear, he heard Ella's voice calling his name. "Hey."

"I just missed picking up the call." She sounded out of breath, and he wondered what she'd been doing. "Sorry. If you left a voicemail, I didn't wait to listen to it. Figured you could just tell me instead."

"I, uh." His words had flowed easily enough when talking to a machine, and he scowled at the tips of his boots. "Wanted to know if you could eat dinner. Would eat. Dinner. With me." He rolled his eyes at his fumbling attempts at the English language. "On a date. Tonight." *Not much better, asshole.*

"Yes." Her laughter was breezy, happy, and somehow he knew the sound wasn't directed at him, but in response to her pleasure at his question. "I'd love to have dinner with you tonight." Her stringing his muddled question into a single statement made him grin. "I could eat."

"Cool, cool." He rolled his eyes again, more frustrated with his fumbling. "I'll pick you up at your house at seven. Dress warmly, yeah?"

"Okay" came her easy response. "I'll see you then, Dawg."

"See you soon, Ella."

And just like that, the hardest phone call he'd ever had was over. It was almost anticlimactic, but at least he'd gotten through the brief exchange. His sense of relief was way out of proportion to the length of the conversation, and he laughed as he blew out a slow breath.

"I'm an idiot."

He didn't even have to think about his agreement with himself.

"Yes, you are."

Chapter Five

Mad Dawg

Rolling to a stop in front of Elodie's house, Mad Dawg glanced down at himself. *Good deal. No bug guts yet.* As per usual, he had on his black leather vest over the jacket. Every time he rode the bike, he flew his colors proudly.

He'd barely put the kickstand down and killed the motor when her front door flew open and Elodie stood there, mouth open wide. With a broad grin she gave him a wave, whirled and petted Chicken, then pushed the dog back as she leaned inside to grab a jacket and slam the door. After double-checking the lock, she shoved her arms into the sleeves of the jacket while she made her way down the short walk, proving she'd listened to his advice to dress warmly.

"We're going riding? I've never done that before." The excitement in her voice was matched by pleasure on her face, and for the first time all day, Mad Dawg felt confident in his decisions for tonight.

"Yeap, come on over and I'll give you the rundown on what to do and expect." He dismounted to meet her beside the bike, and reached one hand to gently push her shining hair out of her face. "First, we'll cover that pretty noggin so I can keep you super safe." Holding up a helmet, he rapped his knuckles against it as he showed it to her. "Good choice of jackets, that one should keep you nice and warm."

She took the helmet from his hands and turned it over, looking at it inside and out. "How does this latch." She fiddled with the straps. "Oh, I see." Positioning it over her head, she paused, then handed it back to him. "Well, shoot. Hold on. Give me a minute." Digging into one jacket pocket, she pulled out a band and began the process of confining her hair. "Okay, now." With the thick locks pulled back into a low ponytail, she stood in front of him and looked up with a broad grin on her face. Spreading her hands in a wide tah-dah motion, she told him, "I'm ready, Dawg."

"Oh, Ella. You are somethin' else." He chuckled. The helmet was a good fit, and he congratulated himself on the pick as he carefully tightened the chin strap. "Lookin' good, woman." Standing back, he gestured to the bike. "Those pegs there are where your feet go. They'll keep you out of the danger zone for the drive shaft or exhaust pipes. Those suckers get hot fast, so it's best to avoid touching them entirely." He slung a leg over the bike and settled himself, then held out his hand for hers. Guiding her into place behind him, he waited for her to wiggle herself comfortable, then grabbed her knees and snugged her a little tighter on the seat. *Queen seat is an apt description.* Shaking off his internal dialog, he directed with, "Feet on the pegs, and your hands around my waist." She made an eager noise, and he grinned as she quickly complied with his orders. "Lean when I lean, and I promise on my life to keep you safe."

"I trust you more than you know." Her chin was propped on his shoulder, made possible by the slightly elevated position of her seat. "You've kept me safe so far. I truly doubt you'd drop the ball now."

"Your lips to God's ears." He started the bike, not surprised when her hands gripped him a little tighter. Turning his head partway around, he caught a glimpse of her shining face. *Not afraid then. It's good she's excited. I love that.* "Ready?" When she nodded, he let the clutch out slowly, rolling them away from the curb.

Before long, they were out of town and onto the country road he'd planned on taking. It wasn't a far ride to the restaurant, but via this route he could stretch it out over a few extra miles with loads of sweeping curves. This would be a good test to see what she really thought of riding the bike.

By the time they got to the place he'd made a reservation, her hands were still holding him tight, but not with a bloodless clutch that would mean she'd become frightened.

Still, he wasn't prepared for her to launch herself at him after they'd dismounted the bike, her arms wrapping around his neck.

"Thank you, thank you, thank you," she whispered against his throat, her mouth moving against his skin in a way that had his cock waking up to say hello. "That was amazing, Dawg. I freakin', freakin' loved it."

"I'm glad, Ella. Means a lot to me." He held her close, his palm stroking up her back until he realized the helmet was still in place. "Here we go. Let's get this off you." She pushed away slightly and lifted her chin, and he chuckled as he unlatched the straps. He twisted to hang it off the handlebars, and when he turned back, she pulled close again. This time her cheek rested against his chest, arms loose around his shoulders. "With that kind of gratitude, I'm gonna go out on a limb and say you didn't hate it."

"God, no. I freakin' loved it." Pulling back, she yanked the tie out of her hair and shook her head once, fluffing it, then grabbed his hand and threaded their fingers together as if the gesture were the most natural thing. "Also, I love, love, love eating at this place. You picked good, Dawg. All the way around. Real good."

With that reassurance, they walked inside and he took the opportunity to wrap an arm around her shoulders as they waited for the host. She leaned against him, head swiveling to look around the restaurant.

"Name on the reservation, please?" The host didn't look up as she thumbed through a book on the stand near the door.

"Dominick Roberts," he said, and Ella immediately shifted closer. He looked down to see her still smiling.

"How is it I just learned your real name right now?" The whisper came with a shimmy of her body. Ella kept her place within the circle of his arm as they started across the dining room. She leaned closer and continued, "Oh wait, it's because I didn't stalk you based on your website."

"Oh, man. I'd argue the point, but that's the unvarnished truth, isn't it?" He pulled a chair out from the table the host indicated, letting her take a seat as he slid it in. "Guilty as charged, ma'am. You caught me. And yeah, that's my government name. My ma calls me Dom, but I like Dawg better. In my eyes, it's more real, as you called it."

"I'm going to need that story one day." She lifted a menu, glancing at both sides before placing it back on the table. "Is it going against every bit of feminism to ask if you'd mind ordering for me?"

"Not that I know," he said, puzzled. "But why? What if I get it wrong?" This seemed like some kind of test, and he wasn't sure how he felt about it.

"Because I think you'll get it right." Folding her hands on top of the menu, she glanced around the room. "You've got all the clues you need, and I'm confident you're one smart cookie. You pay attention, and you've gotten to know me. Just follow your gut. In my experience it never steers a person wrong."

With her reassurance he didn't let his nerves get in the way, instinctively picking out a chicken and pasta dish for her when the waiter came over to take their orders. For his side of the table, he asked for a steak and potatoes meal, which made her smile.

"How'd I do?" Her hands had returned to the table after giving up the menu to the waiter, and he reached out to cover them with his. With her expression, he wasn't foreseeing a negative response, but it'd be nice to know for sure. "Did I get it right?"

"Exactly right. As I expected." She was smiling as she turned one hand over to fit it within his palm. "Now, tell me everything I need to know about you, Dominick Roberts. I feel like I've got some catching up to do."

Their conversation flowed smoothly over dinner, and Mad Dawg was pleased at all the subtle reminders of how easy it was to talk to her. No awkward silences, and she talked as much as he did, which meant it didn't feel like an interrogation. Also, she clearly didn't judge, just listened, and then would add her insights on whatever the topic was. Given their different natures, he found it remarkable how often her viewpoint lined up with his, and he held that knowledge close to his chest.

My do-right-by-people and her karma rules seem to be the same thing. Good to know.

After dinner, they were back in the parking lot, and he waited for her to put her hair up again then secured the helmet for her. He leveraged the excuse of checking the strap to caress her tender throat and she purred, leaning into his touch. Ella climbed on the back of the bike like a pro, slipping up right behind him without a single reminder.

Like it's the most natural thing in the world.

He followed the same route back to town, taking the curves slower, stretching out the time they'd spend together a little longer. They'd barely hit the city limits when a car roared up behind them, bright lights shining in his mirrors. He angled his head to see around the glare and motioned the car ahead with one hand.

Instead of passing him cleanly, the car sped up beside them, slamming back over into his lane with a lurch. Mad Dawg instinctively hit the brakes and pulled the clutch, downshifting as he dropped behind the car. The out of state license caught his eye as the brake lights flashed on, and the car came to a near stop in the middle of the road.

"Sonufabitch," he growled. "What the fuck are these assholes doing?"

With a final squeal of the tires against pavement, the car suddenly took off, the driver giving it a hefty dose of gas.

Picking up speed again, Mad Dawg was careful to keep the bike at a slower than normal pace and turned his head. "You okay?" He looked over his shoulder to see Elodie's pale face.

"I'm okay." She nodded and he patted her hands, still wrapped tightly around his middle.

"Let's get you home."

At the curb in front of her house, he waited for her to dismount before killing the engine and standing. She was removing the helmet with shaky hands and held it out for him to take.

"That whole thing was slightly terrifying. Does it happen often?" She'd taken a step back and he leaned on the bike seat to see what she might do following the traffic encounter.

Might not want anything to do with me now. He hoped he was wrong.

"Not often, no. Those were assholes out to cause trouble."

She gestured at his vest, which had the club's colors proudly displayed on the back. "Was it because of your affiliation? Were they enemies or something? Unscrupulous scoundrels?" Her voice was gradually becoming more certain as she shook off the shock. He was glad to see how quickly she was recovering. *Bodes well for me. Maybe.*

"Not likely. That shit doesn't happen as often as the TV shows make out. Rides are usually scoundrel-free. This was probably kids out joyriding." He took in a deep breath and folded his arms across his chest. "I know you didn't enjoy the ride home as much, but was tonight enough to make you say yes to another dinner?"

Elodie smiled at him, the expression warming as she stepped closer. "I did like the ride home. At least until the immature jerks scared the pants off me. Jerkfaces." Resting a hand on his arm, she slid a little nearer, wedging herself intimately between his spread legs. "And I think I'd say yes to all the dinners you cared to share, I think."

"Yeah? You think?" He quickly uncrossed his arms and touched one hand to her hair, fumbling until he found the restraining band and gently wrangled it free. With one hand on her hip and the other tangled in her hair, he tugged her in a little more. "Well, this is me tellin' you that I'd like to share a lot with you. A whole lot. I don't have to think. I know." He bent close and paused just above her smile-curved lips. "And I'm also asking for more. Officially asking, that is."

She rose to her toes and pressed their lips together for a moment, then backed away an inch, grinning widely. "Want to come inside, Dawg?"

He grimaced and watched the pleasure on her face dim in response. "I hate sayin' this, more than you know, but I'm gonna have to take a raincheck on that, Ella. I've got a couple things to check on tonight."

Her lips twisted in a wry grin. "Okay. We can move at your speed."

"This isn't me not wanting what you're offering." He struggled for words, choosing them carefully to mask that the near-miss tonight might not have been the nothing he'd proclaimed. He needed time to make a couple of calls, see what his brothers thought. *Keeping her safe means taking the hard road sometimes.* His cock gave a pulse in his pants as he took in a lungful of her faint vanilla scent. *Killin' me to do this.* He pushed that certainty into his voice when he told her, "Because I do." Dipping closer, he slid his lips along the line of her jaw, nibbling on her ear. "I really do," he whispered as he mouthed against her skin. "You have no idea, Ella."

"Well, Dawg." She drawled the name out until it filled the air between them. He pulled back and looked down at her, seeing humor in her eyes. "You know where I live. Night."

Darting forward, she captured his mouth again in a quick, hot kiss, then was gone before he could do more than grasp at air. He watched her skip up the walk and through the door, the dog barking a hello to his mistress as the door closed and lights bloomed behind her drapes.

"Dammit," he grumbled, pushing the heel of one hand against his cock as he yanked his phone out. Denver's contact was on his favorites list, and he thumbed the icon with more force than necessary.

Maybe there was a way to salvage his previous plans for the rest of their date.

Maybe.

✳✳✦

Elodie

"Wait," she reminded Chicken, as she changed poses. Moving slowly, she sank into child's pose, big toes touching, knees spread wide. With her arms sagging so the floor supported the entire front of her, Elodie breathed deeply, letting go of the final bits of tension from those terrifying moments of the motorcycle ride.

"Just wait," she told the dog again in a soft whisper when she heard his body move.

He'd greeted her with great enthusiasm when she got home, as he did after absences of sixty seconds or a handful of hours. She'd quickly let him out to do his business, then changed into her leggings and a tight-fitting shirt. Back in the living room, Elodie had put on music resonating at a low hertz conducive to relaxation. From there, it had been the work of moments to flip her mat out and ground her seat bones in easy pose.

Now Chicken had been waiting for nearly thirty minutes, and she knew he was about at the end of his patience.

Eyes closed, it was natural for her to sink into the healing space yoga created within her. She was relaxed and loose, about to sit up and declare herself fair game for Chicken when a knock sounded from the door.

Huffing underneath her breath, she gained her feet, then smiled at the dog, still poised next to the mat.

"Good boy," she praised him, and he bounced up as if on springs. He ran around her and attacked the inside of the front door with both paws, wiggling and wheezing his excitement. That alone told her it was someone he recognized, because it was with nary a bark.

She didn't have any concerns when she pulled the door open and was unsurprised to see Mad Dawg standing there, still bundled in the clothes he'd worn earlier. After all, she'd never heard the bike leave.

"Imagine meeting you here," she joked as she opened the door wider, ushering him through before Chicken could fully attack. On his back legs, Chicken was wiggling madly as he smiled toothily up at Dawg with a lolling tongue. Lifting her chin regally, she proclaimed, "My minion approves of your appearance."

He picked Chicken up effortlessly and rolled the dog to his back in his arms, running a calming hand up the dog's chest and throat. "Well, how does his master feel about it? That's really the burning question here."

"His master also approves," she said in her haughtiest voice, laughing at the end and ruining the effect. "Were you out there this whole time? You should have just come in with me."

"I'm here now. Does that count for something?" He bent to set Chicken on his feet. "Good boy, watchin' out for your momma." The praise was enough to wind the dog up again and he started bouncing on his back feet, front ones planted on Dawg's thigh. "Good boy, be still."

"Off," she instructed, and Chicken stopped jumping and backed up a step. "Good boy. Lava." The dog whirled and took off at a run across the room, jumping over the back of the couch.

"Lava?" Dawg stepped closer to Elodie and the rough callouses on his fingers dragged gently across the skin of her throat. She tilted her chin to give him more access. He smiled down at her as he asked, "What's that command?"

"The floor is lava. Means to get your feet off the floor." She shook her head, reached up and placed a hand to cover his, holding his touch in place. "It's a silly thing, but always makes me laugh." His fingers flexed under hers. "And yes, you being here counts for a lot."

"Good," he murmured as he closed the tiny bit of distance between them. "I'm glad."

Their lips met and she shivered from the blaze of heat that sparked from the contact. "Wow," she whispered, and he nodded slowly, his eyes fractions of an inch away.

"Wow," he agreed softly, then angled his head to kiss her again, this one deeper, longer, and infinitely sweeter. When he pulled back, his lips ghosted across her cheek to her ear to ask, "What were you doing when I knocked?"

Elodie had to shake the cobwebs out of her head. She'd been stunned silent by the force of the connection between them. "Uh, yoga. Relaxation yoga. I do it every night before bed."

"Yeah?" He looped an arm around her waist and steered them around the end of the couch to the open floor. "Got another one of those mat thingies?"

"Does the imaginary bear crap in the hypothetical woods?" She yanked one from a nearby basket, fumbling as she removed the band holding it closed. "I'm the yogi. Of course I do."

Flinging it to the ground, she bent over to arrange the two mats side by side, but not too close. When she straightened, he moved so he was right behind her, and his hands immediately wrapped around her hips, pulling her back against him.

"Gonna teach me yoga, pretty lady?" His words came out muffled as his mouth found the side of her neck. She arched with a stifled mewl, and shivered again as he laughed quietly against her skin. "I'd like that, I think."

"Yes?" The single word came out as a question, so she cleared her throat and repeated, "Yes."

Take that. I'm manifesting I want him to stay the night. Hear me, out there? Stay. The. Night.

"I don't have to wear those tiny leggings, do I?" He dropped another series of kisses against her throat and shoulder. "That might be a deal breaker for me."

She hummed her approval of his caresses, then broke free to take a step back and catch her breath. Clearing her throat a second time, she nodded, then spoke her assent. "Leggings are optional, of course. And yes, I would be pleased to teach you. It's my calling, after all."

His head cocked to one side, then the other. "Calling? Not a job?"

"Oh, gosh, no. The job was in accounting, and I hated every minute." The reminder of how incredibly her life had changed since walking away from the corporate world was enough to sweep the seduction fog from her head. "Now, shall we begin our practice together?" Elodie knelt, then sank so her ass rested on her heels. "If you'd remove your boots and approach the mat, sir?"

This feels like something we might do together every day.

She liked that he was trusting her, letting her take the lead as she had earlier with him and the meal. Not making whatever this was into a competition but leading them together into what could be a partnership.

And there I go, getting ahead of myself. Universe, take what you will from all of this, but make things be happy, okay? I'd appreciate it smuchly. Thanks.

He sat, the chain attached to his wallet rattling loudly. He removed that, then his boots, leaving him in socks. He looked at her with a question and she nodded. "Socks too, you need to feel the grounding as you work."

"Grounding?" Socks tucked into the tops of his boots, he set them to one side and tried to imitate her position. Not unexpectedly, he wasn't as limber as she was, but before he could realize and get self-conscious, she shifted to an easy seated position. "What's grounding?"

"It's the sense of the world around us, the ground cradling us from underneath, the air supporting our efforts. Yoga is taking tiny moments of awareness and stringing them together to create a fabric of relaxation and awareness." Reaching out, she adjusted how his legs were arranged on his mat. "Sounds like a paradox, but it's really not. This position should be more comfortable. It's not about achieving the perfect pose every time, but finding a place within yourself where you can hear your heart, and know things are right with the world." Bringing her hands to heart center, she poised her fingertips together, joining her two hands. With each breath in, she created the illusion of a ball with her fingers, and her exhales deflated it. "Just breathe with me for now. That's more than enough to begin."

He clumsily modeled his hand position after hers, doing the same exaggerated movements with every breath. After a few dozen breaths in and out, she saw his shoulders release slightly, the angle of them dropping down from his ears.

"Good, keep breathing. Try box breathing, now. Count of four in, hold for four, then exhale for four, hold again, and repeat." She demonstrated the process and not surprisingly, he caught on quickly. "The military use this for training in stressful situations."

"This is something I know," he agreed, his voice rumbling as he spoke slowly. His closed eyes and the cadence of his words told her the techniques were working to relax him. "It's familiar."

"Good, familiar is good. It's easy to fall into known routines." She shifted, noting his eyes immediately opened wide, as if he hadn't been aware of closing them. "Let's try a couple of stretches." Feet out in front of her, she propped her body up with arms braced at her back. "Windshield wiper your feet, and let your knees twist only as much as is comfortable. Roll your ankles, let the stress leave your body."

He was slow changing positions, moving as if his body would betray him at any moment. She was well familiar with the sensation, because often once the body accepted a pose it had to be coaxed into the next one.

"Shit's harder than it looks." He winced when he shoved his hands behind him, and she leaned across and tapped his elbow.

"If your wrists hurt at all, go down to your elbows, that way you can give yourself a comfortable angle to work with." She adopted the modified pose, and kept her feet and ankles in motion. "That's better," she said when he sighed into the new position. "Yoga isn't about pain. If something isn't comfortable, there are a thousand ways to change a pose. That's why it's called a practice, because we're always refining."

"Kinda like life." His head dropped back naturally, and she took a moment to stare openly at him as he looked up at the ceiling. "When shit doesn't fit, then find your niche and make it your home. Like me with the shop."

"Yes, exactly like that." She held the position for another ten breaths, then sat upright, resting her palms on her thighs. "Let's try a hinge stretch. Sit up tall, ground your seat bones to the mat, and let your body sag forwards naturally. Move your glutes out of the way like this." She pulled the large muscles towards the back of her butt, settling better onto the mat. "Now, let your back round. Get comfortable. It shouldn't hurt anywhere, but there will be a pull at the backs of your legs and your low back. Breathe natural to your own rhythm. Just go lax. Focus your inward breath where there's tension, and blow it out, the heat of that stretch leaving your body with your breath."

He continued using the box breathing method and she smiled down at her knees. *He's a good student.*

"Don't worry how far you can stretch. If it's more comfortable, prop your forehead on your fists like this." She demonstrated, and then reached out to wrap a hand around each ankle. "Or you can put your hands on your knees or shins, or on the mat beside your legs. However feels good, that's what you need to pursue."

"It's definitely a stretch." His voice was thin and she turned her head to look at him, watching as he rolled a shoulder. "Doesn't hurt, but I can feel it everywhere. Not just my legs and back."

"Good." Her short answer drew a chuckle from him. "Means you're doing it right."

They held that for a few more breaths, and she counted them out of the pose. "And one, relax." He sat up, rolling both shoulders this time. "Let's stretch out our spines. Move to your back and bring your legs to your chest. If that's uncomfortable or awkward, lie on your side and tuck your knees into a fetal position. As best as you can." She demonstrated both positions, staying on her side when he adopted that pose. "Feel the muscles of your back release. Tuck your tailbone under, let your glutes stretch everything back into place."

"This isn't too bad," he offered, lying an arm's length away, eyes closed and a relaxed expression on his face. "I sure don't hate it."

"Final shavasana, it's called corpse pose, and it's my favorite. That's because, no matter how hard my practice was, when I hit this one, I know I'm done for the night." She rolled to her back. "Legs out long, tuck your shoulder blades under your back, so there's a natural arch in your neck. Arms down to your sides, and let your feet relax outward. Palms up to receive, and simply breathe. We'll stay here as long as needed."

Eyes closed, she listened as he adjusted, then shifted a couple of times before growing quiet. The music was playing in the background, a soft accompaniment to the ending of this joint yoga session.

Elodie drew in a long breath, and blew it out, pleased when he did the same. Then, for two or three minutes, they simply lay on their mats, quiet, unspeaking.

She rolled to one elbow and opened her mouth to tell him how well he'd done, but quickly decided to keep her observations to herself.

Dawg was sleeping on her floor, head cocked to one side as if he'd been keeping an eye on her. *Watchin' out for me.*

Elodie grinned and lay back down, closer this time, and hooked her little finger around his. *Puttin' it out there that I like this. Thanks, universe. Appreciate this gift you've sent my way.*

She'd wait for him to wake.

***

Mad Dawg

Groaning, he yawned and stretched, the bed unfamiliar and uncomfortable underneath him.

"Sleeping handsome awakes." Soft lips brushed against his cheek and he smiled as he recognized the voice and rolled towards Ella, opening his eyes.

"Was I supposed to do that?" Blinking sleep from his eyes, he stared at her. "Relax that much?"

"It's not something I encourage at the studio, for obvious reasons." She shifted to lay her head on one folded arm. Bringing his hand to her mouth, she gently kissed the back of it. "But here? A short catnap is entirely appropriate."

"How long was I out?" He looked beyond her at Chicken on the couch, snoring with all four feet in the air. "You stayed with me?"

"Not long, a few minutes. Maybe thirty." Fingers threaded through his, she tucked his hand underneath her cheek. "And yeah, I took the opportunity to relax just a little longer, too."

"These mats aren't meant for napping." Stretching out his legs, he groaned as muscles twinged. "Not a bed, that's for sure."

"Nope, they're one-use, really. They have thicker mats for folks who have knee problems. Makes it easier to kneel in various poses, but even those aren't a substitute for a good bed." Her smile widened, growing mischievous. "And I happen to have a very good bed."

"Do tell?" He twisted to look at the speaker next to the TV. The pulses of sound came at regular intervals, resonating through his ears. "What the hell is this music? I think it's hypnotic or something. I can't believe I fell asleep."

"It's not music per se. It's a set of tones, ones specifically tuned for relaxation. Your body knows what it needs, and this is a tool to open the door. If I'd used essential oils too, I doubt you'd have woken before morning." She curled a little closer, eyes dancing with amusement. "I told you I'm a master at my craft."

"I'll never doubt you again, woman." He stretched and was gratified to hear several vertebrae in his back pop and crack. "Best sleep I've had in a while. Even short, it was really good."

"And the yoga? You didn't hate it?" She echoed his words about the ride from earlier. The expression on her face told him she already knew the answer.

Grinning wryly, he told her, "I liked it. I'm not an idiot, though. I know you took it easy on me. But it was a nice introduction." He angled his head to bring his lips to hers, brushing across once, twice, three times before he pulled back. "This was nice."

"Yeah. It really was."

Chicken snorted in his sleep and rolled to his belly on the couch, blinking down at Mad Dawg for a moment before his face expanded into a doggy grin.

Mad Dawg barely got his hands down to protect his balls before the dog leaped on him.

"Chicken Nugget. No," Elodie scolded through her laughter. "Stop it. Off, you beast. Off."

Face wet from doggie kisses, Mad Dawg fell to his back, laughing.

"Even with nearly getting nutted by Chicken, this is nice."

His phone buzzed, the normally quiet sound seeming loud in the relaxed atmosphere. Before he could fish it out of his pocket, it buzzed again, then a third time. The smile faded from Elodie's face, morphing into a regretful expression before he could even look at the device.

"It was nice," she echoed his words, with a change that signified she understood the summons likely meant he'd be leaving.

The messages were from Denver, and even without reading them, Mad Dawg knew they had to do with the traffic altercation from earlier. He sat, bent his knees, and propped an elbow on each, phone dangling from one hand.

"Ella—I—" He stopped, not sure how to continue. He knew what he needed to say, but his mouth was entirely reluctant to voice the words.

"My bed will be here. I'm not giving it away." She leaned forward and covered his hand with hers, the warmth and contact a comfortable gesture, as if they'd touched like this for a hundred years. "When the time's right, things will fall into place for us to be together."

"When the time's right?" Clasping her hand, he drew Ella to him, arranging her limbs in his lap. As she nestled against his chest, Mad Dawg found himself hating the need to leave. This wasn't like anything he'd known in the past. "Ella, you're one of a kind. You know that, right?"

Her fingers ruffled his short beard, tugging his chin down to press her lips against his. "What a wonderful compliment." Arms wrapped around her back, he tugged her closer as she wound her arms around his neck. "Thank you."

"Oh, darlin'. You are no hardship to be around, trust me. I wouldn't twist myself into a pretzel for just anybody, you know what I mean?"

She laughed in the middle of their next kiss and he captured the sound in his mouth, dipping his tongue inside to glide against hers.

They were both breathing heavily when the phone buzzed again, breaking them apart to stare down at the device dancing across the floor.

"I should go," he said reluctantly, and she nodded, her hair brushing against his shoulder.

"Just be sure you come back." Shifting to her knees, she loomed over him, hands cradling his face. "I kinda like you, Dawg."

He pressed a tiny kiss against the tip of her thumb tracing across his lips.

"I kinda like you, too."

Chapter Six

Elodie

The midmorning class was just filing out the front door when Elodie heard the back door handle jiggle. She waved goodbye to the last chatty member and bent to swipe a discarded towel from the floor as she turned.

She froze, the happy greeting for Dawg stuck in her throat, towel twisted in her hands.

It wasn't him. The larger of the two men stalking inside looked a lot like one of Dawg's friends who'd watched over her last week, but the other man was unfamiliar. Every hair on her body lifted as she went on high alert.

"Hi." She hated the tones of uncertainty in her voice and pushed more strength into her next words. *Never show fear.* That had been a hard-learned lesson, but one that she instinctively knew was important to heed right now. "Did Dawg send you?"

"Rich, fuckin' rich to think that," the stranger drawled. "No, bitch, Dawg didn't send us. The fuck?"

"Shut up," the other man said, and for a moment, Elodie wasn't certain whether it was aimed at her or the stranger. "Bitches should be fucked and not heard."

Guess that clears that up. The men's attitudes reeked of arrogance and confidence. *They're not friends of his.* Every warning reminder from Mad Dawg rolled through her mind, and she winced at the knowledge she hadn't locked the back door this morning. *Basic safety 101 and I failed.*

"What do you need?" She gestured towards Dawg's shop through the wall, stalling for time as she tried to come up with a graceful way out of whatever this was. "He's not open yet."

"Fuckin' got eyes, don't I?" The stranger approached, one foot in front of the other, padding towards her like a big cat. Each step eroded some of her forced poise. She straightened her spine, refusing to show weakness in front of them. "Whole reason I rolled my ass out of bed this fuckin' early."

"You're gonna wanna come quiet. Won't go well for you if you don't." This man, the one she thought she recognized, went to the alarm panel as if he'd been here a thousand times. Flipping open the panel, he punched in a series of numbers. "Okay, we've got about a minute. Let's get her packaged and out of here."

She had been backing towards the front door, gauging how quickly she'd be able to get to and through the opening. *If I can just get outside, I'll be in the clear.* It would be a couple hours before Mad Dawg opened his shop, but there were other businesses nearby. She glanced away from the men for a moment, gaze taking in the empty parking lot. More clients should be arriving soon for the next class. *Safety, just through the glass.*

The first man, the stranger, rushed at her, dropping one shoulder so he scooped her up and head down over his back. Elodie screamed, fighting with everything inside her until a blinding pain surrounded her head, and everything she could hear was suddenly far away and echocy. "Help," she yelled, wincing at how the sound amplified the pain in her head. "Help me, please."

"Shut her the fuck up."

That was the last thing she remembered hearing for a long time.

***

Mad Dawg

Gliding to a stop behind the building, Mad Dawg parked his bike next to Ella's car. He looked around, angry and disappointed that the prospect he'd called wasn't still standing guard. Didn't matter that the sun was well past daybreak, his instructions had been extremely specific, up to and including the time between when the man would see Ella safe into her studio, and when Mad Dawg would arrive.

"Goddammit," he grumbled under his breath, standing next to the bike and opening the saddlebag to pull out the small bag of donuts he'd picked up. "Tell a man his job, make sure he understands he's got one job, and he still fucks it up."

He was letting himself into the shop when he heard a soft sound, not quite a groan, but nothing he could blame on the wind, either. Kicking a piece of brick into the gap to prop the door open, he set down the donuts, emptying his hands, and turning to take a cautious step down the alley.

Now that he was away from the doors, he picked out the shape of a motorcycle parked partly behind the dumpsters.

"The fuck?" Every sense in overdrive, Mad Dawg kept close to the brick wall as he approached, his eyes landing on a clothing-covered lump on the ground. "Jesus Christ," he muttered, sinking down on one knee next to the laid-out prospect. His fingers found a slowly bleeding wound on the back of his head, which told a story, but it wasn't one Mad Dawg wanted to hear. Yanking his phone out of his pocket, he hit Rocker's number.

When the man answered with a "Yo" Mad Dawg barked, "Trouble at the shop." Not waiting for a response, he terminated the call and deposited the phone deep in his pocket. Rolling the prospect to the side elicited a moan, and he noticed multiple contusions on the man's hands.

"Didn't go down easy," he commented softly, one hand on the man's chest. His heart was beating steadily, which was good. "Good for you." He patted softly. "Be right back, brother. You did good."

Regaining his feet he moved quickly, sweeping through the rest of the alley. Music came from Ella's studio, and he assumed a class was in session. Not wanting to interrupt her business, he worked his way methodically through all the nooks and crannies where an attacker could be hiding. By the time Rocker and three more men arrived, he'd ensured his shop was also clear, front and back.

"What the fuck happened?" Rocker's demand echoed the feeling of unease Mad Dawg felt.

"No idea. He was down when I got here. The alley's clear, and there's nobody in my shop. Nothing's out of place other than the prospect laid out on his back." He gestured to the man. "He's starting to vocalize, which means he's coming out of it. I don't think he's been out long. Head's still bleeding. If it was hours, it would have clotted by now."

"You think it's HHMC? Jesus. Okay, what next?" Rocker stood next to Mad Dawg's bike, looking up and down the alley.

"I'm gonna check on Ella quick."

Leaving the other men to tend to the prospect, Mad Dawg went to Ella's back door and knocked loudly. He could still hear the music going inside, but she should hear him easily. Turning around to survey the alley again, he became uneasy when there was no answer. Her car *was* here. Another round of knocking delivered the same results and it suddenly dawned on him he'd seen a small crowd of women at the front door as he'd rode in. Waiting patiently as if the door to the studio were locked, which shouldn't be the case if Ella was here.

"Rocker, here." Movement behind him assured him his brother would have his back. "I've got a bad feeling."

Fist curling around the knob on the back door, he held his breath and twisted, blowing out a steady stream when it turned easily in his hand.

"Goddammit, it's unlocked." He didn't bother whispering, because if Ella hadn't responded to his pounding, she sure wouldn't be bothered by a conversation. "I'm going in."

He held it for a count of two, then flung it wide, stepping inside and moving laterally to the door, crouching against the back wall of her studio. The door struck the wall and rebounded, but not before he saw what was beyond it.

Nothing.

Nothing except her empty studio.

The alarm started beeping as if it were still set for overnight, threatening to bring the cops.

"Where is she?" Rocker asked, leaning against the door, holding it open. "What the fuck is going on, Mad Dawg?"

"Your guess is as good as mine, brother." Mad Dawg opened the panel and a piece of paper fell out. He caught it and then quickly pressed the sequence of keys to disarm the alarm. Unfolding the paper, he saw the message first, "Want her back?" It was followed by a hand-drawn map, indicating a location outside town. It also held a small square of what felt like plastic. When he turned that over, he found it was an instant photo. Ella was in the image, limbs carelessly arranged in what looked like a car's trunk. Her eyes were closed, and he could see bruising already developing along her temple. Blood oozed from her nose across her upper lip.

"Brother, what'd you find?" Rocker's question didn't matter.

Nothing mattered.

Nothing except the image of Elodie, graceless in a way she never was, not even in her sleep.

Mad Dawg didn't look away from the picture, couldn't tear his gaze away. Each ragged breath was like knives stabbing his throat. He felt rather than saw Rocker approach his shoulder and shoved the note his direction, keeping the image in front of himself.

This can't be how things shake out. I can't lose her. I've just fuckin' found her, goddammit.

"Holy fuck, man. They took your Ella?" The anguish in Rocker's voice echoed the pain building in Mad Dawg's chest.

That was the truth, wasn't it? She was his Ella, and these motherfuckers had taken her. Put their hands on her. Bloodied and bruised her. *My Ella. Fuckin' mine.*

"They're gonna pay." The words gritted from between his teeth, jaw clenched tight to stop the screams threatening to escape. "I'm gettin' her back right the fuck now. Motherfuckers did the exact wrong thing."

"Goddamn right they did. Doesn't matter who they are, they're gonna figure out they've kicked the wrong beehive. Hold tight, though. Let me make a couple of calls. We'll get some more brothers over here. Hold it together, my friend." Rocker bumped his shoulder. "You need to flip her sign to closed? Let the pretty biddies outside know she's sick or some shit?"

His back was to the front of her studio, but glancing up at the reflection in the mirrors showed him what Rocker was talking about. There were probably twenty women standing on the front walk, waiting. A few of them had cupped their hands to try and see through the sunscreen film.

"Yeah." He clenched his hands, careful not to crease the photo. *My Ella.* "Fuck, man, no, I can't do that. I can't talk to them. Don't think I can talk to anybody. Fuck. I'm not together enough. Can you, brother? Can you take care of it?"

"You betcha," Rocker responded immediately, clapping a hand to Mad Dawg's bicep as he walked past, towards the front door. "Ladies, ladies, I've got some bad news for you." The rattle of the door closing cut off his words, but in the reflection, Mad Dawg could see the women drifting away. Except for a couple who'd clustered closer to Rocker.

Motherfucker will probably come away from this with digits. He wanted to be angry at Rocker, but every bit of his emotion was focused on the motherfuckers who'd taken his Ella.

He looked at the picture again, this time focusing on everything he could see that *wasn't* Elodie.

Gotta think. Gotta find her.

Gray car paint, gray carpeting inside the trunk. The shape of the trunk said sedan, and the gleam of the bumper indicated it was relatively new. The carpeting wasn't dirty or stained, and there was a little sticker to one side. He looked closer, making out a cleaning company logo. Probably rented, then. The license wasn't in the image, though. *Fucking hell.*

Rocker appeared back beside him. "All locked up, brother. Told them she'd fallen ill, and would post on her website if she couldn't make other classes. Covered."

"Look at this." Mad Dawg shoved the image towards Rocker. "It's a fucking rental, Rocker. Dammit. I mean, a rental? Fuck, that's just great. Great. We're looking for a gray sedan, rental. There's gotta be a thousand of those on the roads around here."

"Maybe, but maybe not. It's something. Pair that with the fuckin' map, and we might have enough to find out who." Rocker turned the image over to inspect the back. "It's one of those portable instant photos. There's not many of those around here. Smaller than a regular Polaroid. I wonder if there's a local place to buy the film? We can look for that too."

"Look for photo paper? I don't think it's just anyone off the street. You were right when you called out the HHMC. Who the fuck would do this if not those assholes?" Mad Dawg shook his head. "No, they somehow figured out she was important to me and decided to hit me where it'd hurt the most. It's them, dammit. *Fuck.* They could have firebombed the shop and insurance woulda taken care of everything. No, they took something that can't be replaced."

"Yeah, but we know the entirety of the HHMC aren't fucknuggets. I'm betting it's one single, ambitious motherfucker who's decided you're how he's going to make his patch. They've got a different process than us, we know that." Rocker rested one closed fist on Mad Dawg's shoulder, pounding gently. He shrugged away, not wanting the reassurance. "Hell, it's different from most clubs. I guess when your focus is on dragging in the most money, any way, any how, it'll also be the focus for members. Ain't right, what they do, but that's their business. It has been, at least. Until it crosses paths with us."

"Jesus. They got Ella, man. I don't care if some asshole's lookin' to buy his officer patch with a donation. All I want is her back safe." He shoved the picture into his pocket, hands clenching into fists, nails digging half-moon craters in his palms. Cold, trembling with rage, Mad Dawg fought to hold it together. Images of her filled his mind, the brilliance of her remembered smile failing to warm him. "I gotta get her back, Rocker. I need her back." His heart pounded in his ears, nearly deafening him.

"Same, brother. We all want her safe. But we gotta be smart about it. We also want you safe." Rocker's fingers dug into the leather of Mad Dawg's vest, pulling tight and stopping him when he would have walked away.

"You son of a bitch, let me go. Fuck what happens to me. I don't care. I just gotta get her back." He leaned closer, voice raising to an angry shout. "She's fuckin' mine, man. Mine." He slapped a palm against his chest, covering the spot where she loved to rest her cheek. "She's mine. And they've got her."

A rumble of motorcycles died in the alley and the back door opened a moment later, Tinder walking through. "What do we know?"

Rocker released Mad Dawg and reached out a hand, clasping Tinder's while Mad Dawg stood stock still, fingers again curled into fists. If he moved, he was afraid he'd fall to pieces, shattered by the threat of loss. *She's mine, and everyone better fucking understand. I'll do anything needed to get her back.*

"Tell me, brother." Tinder's hand landed on Mad Dawg's shoulder.

He pulled in a harsh breath and held it for a count of four, then blew it out slowly. *Box breathing, like I did with her. Hold on, Ella. For God's sake, hold on.* "Ella's studio was unlocked, alarm still set, but her car's out back. None of my shit was bothered. Nothing else is out of place. It's them, Tinder. It's gotta be HHMC. They took Ella and left a note with a map. They must have clocked the prospect outside and took him down, but he'll be okay. He was waking up when the guys got here. Cage was likely a rental. Looks to be a nondescript gray sedan. But I don't know what they want. They took her and then just left the map, brother." His hands started shaking and he squeezed his eyes closed. "But they've got my Ella, man. They've got her." Opening his eyes to stare at Tinder, he willed his friend and brother to understand. "My Ella."

Tinder looked over the note and photo, then handed them to Rocker as he stared at Mad Dawg from underneath his brows. "We know it's HHMC for sure? A scribbled piece of paper and a picture? That's it? Nothing else? Nothing at your shop? Fuck, man, this isn't much. We need more before we start a war."

"Yeah," Rocker agreed, and Mad Dawg shot a venom-filled glare at him. Fury boiled through his veins at what felt like betrayal.

He shook his head, rejecting their flawed thinking. "You don't understand, man. I don't need more. It's enough for me. There's a fuckin' map, man. It's not up for discussion. Jesus Christ, I'll walk in and trade myself for her if I need to."

"The fuck you will, man." Tinder shook his head, gaze softening. "Mad Dawg, trust us. If they took her, you and I both know they won't just let her go, brother. If it is them, you go in there like that, and it'd be the two of you in the HHMC hands then."

"The map alone is enough." He angled away to reach for the paper as Rocker yanked it back. "Motherfucker, give that back."

"Half a minute, brother. Trust." Tinder's voice was low, and when Mad Dawg looked at him, the expression on his face had turned grim. "We're all workin' on it. Every one of us. We got people coming in. I agree with you that it's likely HHMC. And I agree that this cannot go unanswered. But this will be war, man. *War*. I get it. They took your woman by force, and that's a fuckin' tragedy besides bein' scary as hell. Brother, you gotta think with your head. I don't wanna do this more than once. That means when we get the info needed we'll hit them, and we'll fuckin' do it with force. No solo runs. Zero chances of fuckin' up. We can't risk that. Not with your woman in their hands. No goddamned do-overs here."

"You see the picture, Tinder? Did you fuckin' see?" His chest tightened until he had to force the words out between stuttered breaths. When he reached for Tinder's vest, it was with trembling hands. "They put their goddamned hands on her."

"I saw it, brother. And I hear you, man. Loud and clear. But give me half a minute." Tinder leaned his forehead against Mad Dawg's. "I'd never put her at risk without reason."

"I know. I know that in my head. I do." Eyes burning, he squeezed them tightly closed. "But fuck, man. *Fuck*. We nearly got run off the road last night." His eyes popped open at the memory. "Jesus Christ, man. Just last night, here in town, and it was a goddamned gray sedan. There's gotta be cameras caught that shit."

"Yup, there was. You called in that bullshit, which means we pulled the footage last night before it got overwritten. Denver's still racing through it right now. And he's pulled video from this morning too. We're just waiting on his call."

"Jesus. I thought they were just after me last night. Never fuckin' crossed my mind they'd have picked Ella instead."

"Might have saved her life, you hangin' out with her so late." Tinder gave him a cynical grin. "Sucks you had club business that pulled you away, but you and me are guaranteed that the prospect out there did his dead level best to keep her safe."

"Yeah, I saw the condition of his hands." Mad Dawg pulled in a rough breath, his body vibrating as anxiety and adrenaline warred in his body. "Jesus, Tinder. I don't know how much longer I can wait, brother."

Tinder's phone gave a ting, followed by a repeated series of the sounds, and then rang as he was pulling it out. Instead of answering the call, he flipped to the text messages, sliding his thumb across the screen to move through the images. "Got them." After that satisfied pronouncement, he lifted the phone and redialed the last call. "Yo, Denver, saw it all. Looks good, my brother. Looks really fuckin' good. Got any news on that location from the map? Uh-huh. Yeah, I hear ya. Yeah. Okay, got that too. Send it to the group. Thanks, man. Good work."

As Tinder disconnected the call, Mad Dawg crowded close. "What? What'd he send? What'd he say?"

"Map location is bogus. Likely an ambush setup to have your ass picked up. He got a good address, though, because the motherfucker who rented the car is a stupid dumbass who used his real information. Denver pulled more footage from close to the second address and confirmed the fuckin' car is sittin' bold as brass in the trailer's driveway, and there are three bikes parked in a lean-to nearby."

"What are we doing still standing here, then? Let's go."

A member stuck his head through the studio back door and looked around. "Mad Dawg, there's a dude just came in over at the shop and said he's got information for you. Pounded on the door until we let him in."

"Let's see what whoever it is has to say," Tinder said, giving Mad Dawg a shove towards the door. "Come on. Won't be but half a minute."

"Everything with you is half a minute," he griped, giving way to the steering hands of these men he trusted with his life. *With Ella's life.* The realization steadied him. If Tinder felt there was enough time to divert for a moment, he'd go along with it. *For now.*

In his shop, Martini stood, staring down a three-pack of RMMC members who were between him and the front door. When Mad Dawg walked in the back, Martini turned and glared at him.

"Hey, man. Hey, I wanted to let you know about those two guys who were in here the other day. I saw them again." He shuffled his feet. "They were putting gas in a car. Thumping fists on the trunk and laughing. I thought I heard a woman scream. When I started walking their way, they jumped in and drove off, yanked the gas handle from the pump and left with the rubber dragging behind them. Seemed important, like something you should know."

"Did you see where they went?" Mad Dawg straightened. If Ella was in the trunk at the time, aware and able to yell, then she might yet be okay. "Follow them?"

"Yeah, from a ways behind, but I stayed with them. They stopped at a trailer over in the manufactured housing village out east of town. Second drive, and they're in the third trailer house down." He shrugged tightly. "I'd hazard a guess that from the studio being closed who it is they have. I'm—" He hesitated, then straightened his shoulders, lifting his chin. "Mad Dawg, if you need another set of hands, I'm down for helping you."

"Appreciate it, brother." Mad Dawg traveled the couple of steps separating them, then pulled Martini into a close clinch. The pounding on his shoulder lent him strength. "Means a fuck of a lot."

"Sure thing. You should ride with us. If our brother Mad Dawg speaks for you, ya gotta be a good'un, for sure." Tinder spoke up. "It'd be a blessing in disguise to find a good man out of this."

Mad Dawg released Martini and spun to face Tinder, hands balled into fists once again.

"You fuckin' call it a blessing again and I'd like to see what happens to your face." Rocker spoke up, throwing an arm over Tinder's shoulder and pulling him out of reach. He held out a placating palm to Mad Dawg. "From the expression our brother's wearin', I'm guessin' it'll be a while before Mad Dawg sees eye-to-eye with you on that."

"Can we fuckin' roll now? Get the hell outta here?" Mad Dawg turned and strode towards the door, glad when he heard the tromping of boots coming behind him. "We have a location, now also positively confirmed by an outside source, and these motherfuckers have already done enough." Pushing through the door, he scanned the alley, surprised at the number of men who'd ridden in while they were inside the shop. *There's gotta be a hundred Maniacs here. For me. For Ella.* He pulled in a deep breath and greeted them all with a lift of his chin. *My brothers.*

"I've got a group headed to the bogus location they gave you, too," Tinder said as he threw a leg over his bike parked next to Mad Dawg's. "Figured we might as well sweep up everything in one motion."

"Don't fuckin' care," Mad Dawg muttered as he thumbed the ignition on his bike. "Do not fucking give a good goddamn about that." His pipes roared as he rolled the throttle. He shouted over the rattle of noise, "All I fuckin' care about is Ella. Safe and sound, please, God."

He knew the exact location Martini had pinpointed, and the target for his rage was only a couple of miles away. Fighting every instinct that told him to rocket along the roads, he kept to a sedate pace, working up and down through the gears as he traveled through green lights, Tinder on his left shoulder, Rocker right behind. The rest of the men were strung out in two columns behind them. Mad Dawg knew that the last thing they needed was to get pegged by the cops racing to the rescue. It would delay them way more than riding normally. This way it'd just look like a group of them out for a midday ride, and nothing more.

It would chap Tinder's ass to not have a plan already laid out for their arrival, but Mad Dawg didn't need one. His goal was simple. To the point.

Get in. Get Ella. Kill the fuckers.

Uncaring of the sound of the bikes, he pulled into the drive Martini had mentioned. He motioned for Rocker to take the next, so he would come up the other end of the big, sweeping U-shaped street.

Them knowing we're here won't change a fuckin' thing.

Kickstand down, he killed the bike and unsnapped his pistol's holster with a quick flick of his wrist. He could pull it from the small of his back in a fraction of a second, and would if needed.

They put their fuckin' hands on Ella. I won't hesitate a moment to end their asses.

From inside the trailer, he heard loud yelling, both male and female voices. Unable to make out the words, he still recognized Ella's angry screams just as a hand drew back the curtain over the window on the door.

Pausing before the aged trailer, he gave the door handle a hard yank, breaking the latch and pulling it wide open. In one leap, he jumped past the couple of stacked cinderblocks that served as steps. The man who'd been checking through the window was standing in the middle of the room, hands submissively up by his ears.

"He's cutting her loose now," the man shouted, face pale. "Jesus, please don't kill me. It wasn't my idea. None of this shit was my idea. Jesus."

Ella stumbled out of the hallway to the left, tumbling and going to her knees on the dirty kitchen linoleum. She yelled wordlessly, face red with anger, then swung her head and saw Mad Dawg. In an instant, she had regained her feet and was in his embrace, clinging to him like a spider monkey. Her arms were tight around his neck, nearly choking, but he didn't care. He quickly stepped to the side to give his brothers room to come in and let himself focus on her, trusting them to do what was needed.

"Baby," he crooned, mouth close to her ear. "Ella, baby. My Ella. Are you okay?" His hands slipped up and down her arms, feeling for injuries. He cupped the curve of her skull and pulled back slightly with difficulty. She didn't want to let go her hold on him. When he could see her face, his breath caught at the bruising at the side of her head. It was darker than in the photo, purple spreading along her brow and over her ear. Dried blood marked her jaw and neck, a smear of brighter scarlet along her upper lip. Cold fury infused him. *Put their fuckin' hands on her. Bastards are gonna pay.* "Baby, tell me you're okay."

"I didn't know what to do." Her eyes lifted and their gaze met. Her pupils dilated widely, and she started shaking. Her visceral terror built the rage already bubbling inside him higher. The idea she'd gone through all of this because of him was a cold weight in the center of his chest. "I'm okay. I think I'm okay. I just kept yelling and yelling, hoping someone would hear me."

"You did just right, baby. Just right. Someone did hear you. Brought me here. You did good, Ella." He gathered her to his chest again, rocking her back and forth slowly, trying to calm them both. "Everything, just right."

"My studio," she gasped, pulling away. "They took me from there. I don't know what they did to it."

"Nothing. They didn't do anything other than lock the front door. It's all okay, baby. Everything's going to be okay."

No matter what it takes, I'll make it right. The only thing I can't handle is not having her. Whatever is needed, I'll make it right.

"It's going to be okay," he reassured them both, praying it was the truth.

***

Elodie

Heart still racing, ears ringing with adrenaline, Elodie doubted it would be okay as easily as Dawg declared.

She had to admit it was really good to be held tightly in his arms right now. And to know she'd been correct.

I knew he'd come.

This had been the second most frightening thing she'd ever endured. Part of the fear had been tied up in not knowing what was coming next. More had been in the fact it had been bikers who'd taken her hostage. *Kidnapped me. Took me.* Even before they'd gotten to the trailer, she'd been certain they weren't Mad Dawg's friends, not in his club, because the patches didn't match. Which had left the men in the no man's land of potentially foe. *Most definitely foe.* While tied up in the bedroom, she'd overheard one of the men talking about the encounter on the road the previous night, and that had told her everything she'd needed to know. *Bad guys.*

The only thing that kept her sane had been the knowledge that if Mad Dawg knew what they'd done, he'd come find her. She'd believed that, deep down in her soul. The connection they shared wouldn't let him do anything else.

I was right. I was right, and he called me his Ella. He'll always be there for me.

She snuggled against him a little tighter, trying to calm the trembling in her limbs. Slowing her breathing didn't help much, but it eased the ringing somewhat. Knowing this was an adrenaline drop didn't change how it all made her feel. Vulnerable in a way she hadn't allowed in years. Elodie shook her head, trying to drive the ancient memories away. From the first moment they'd put their hands on her today, things had been out of her control, and now her mind and body were betraying her.

"Baby," he murmured, lips soft against the side of her head. "I wanna get you home."

"And I wanna go home, so we're in agreement. Please, Dawg." She blinked at the bright lights, then closed her eyes against the smears of color. "Can someone lock my shop?"

"Already handled," he reminded her.

"Oh, yeah. Sorry." She leaned her head against his chest, his arms a solid comfort against her back. *He's got me. He'll keep me safe.* "Can you take me home?"

"I got the bike with me." He paused, then continued less certainly, "I can have someone bring a car if you want."

"No, Dawg. I'll ride with you." Rearing back, leaning against his strong arms, she looked him in the face. His expression changed as his gaze explored what must be spectacular bruising if the rage emoted was anything to judge by. It sure hurt like it was bad. "I'm safe with you. Always safe with you." His face softened as she echoed her thoughts, and he raised a hand to cup the side of her face not bruised. *Maybe he needs the reassurance too.* "I was so scared when I woke up in the trunk of the car. Scared out of my mind. All I could think of was that you'd take care of me. I knew you'd come. I knew it."

"God, woman." The words were filled with gravel as he gathered her close again, his embrace strong but oh-so tender. "You fuckin' kill me. Slay me with your trust."

"I'm safe with you," she repeated, eyes closing with relief. "Take me home."

Chapter Seven
Mad Dawg

They dismounted the bike in front of her house, and Ella looked left and right at the two men who had trailed them here.

"If they want, I can make coffee or something for everyone?" She winced as she removed the helmet, a flash of pain creasing her brow as she handed it to him. He hung it off the handlebars. "If they're staying?"

His brothers had parked and killed their bike engines, but looked to him before dismounting.

"Nope, their place is out here. We just need to verify for certain that there aren't any other threats hiding in the bushes. It's an overabundance of caution, I promise. Regardless, they'll take care of the outside, and I'll check inside." Need burned inside him to ensure she was safe. The terror from realizing she'd been taken hadn't faded yet. "Make sure."

She turned to look down the street. "It's unlikely anyone would hide out here, especially in broad daylight."

"And I'd have thought it unlikely they'd have come to your studio. Never would have thought they'd—" He pressed his palm flat against her low back, biting back the words as he urged her towards the house. *I need to get her inside. Out of view. Out of danger.* "Let me take care of you, baby. We're better safe than sorry, at least for now."

Inside, Ella dropped to a knee to greet Chicken, then folded her legs to sit on the floor without being asked. *Good girl,* he thought.

On high alert, Mad Dawg moved into the building using the skills learned in the military, throwing open doors and looking in corners. He found nothing, which was a good thing all around. His breathing slowed down gradually as he cleared the house. When he returned to the front room, Ella had removed her shoes and was crooning to the dog. It looked and felt so natural, the rest of the day was surreal in contrast. *Probably be a while before I'm back to normal. Before we're back to normal.*

Chicken seemed to sense something, spending a long time sniffing her face and hands, all along her pants, and then back to her face. The dog gave her a swipe of the tongue along one cheek and Ella laughed, then winced and grabbed at the side of her head.

"Everything's clear in here. Are you all right?" He grabbed her hand, tugging her up and against his side, needing the weight and heat of her body to help ground him. *She's safe.* The idea of what might have happened if he'd been unable to find her was like acid burning through his brain. So much could have gone wrong. *But it didn't, and she's here now. Safe.* He just had to keep remembering that truth.

"Got a bit of a headache," Ella admitted as she stood.

"Not surprising. I think I'd be more shocked if it didn't hurt, way they walloped you." Wanting to take care of her, he gestured deeper inside the house as he toed off his boots. "Point me to where you keep your painkillers, and I'll gather stuff. You want to rest on the couch, or in your bedroom?" He made to step away, then paused when her hand landed on his arm. "Yeah, baby?"

"Depends." The smile she gave him was shaky, tentative. "Will you still be here?"

He swept her into his arms gently, holding her close. "Baby, I'm not going any-fucking-where. Couldn't pry me loose with a crowbar. I'm here, with you, and there's nowhere else I want to be." The unvarnished truth seemed to please her, because the tiny smile grew to a wide grin that lasted until she winced again. "Let me get you something for your head, baby. Get you settled so we can both rest, yeah?"

"Kitchen, third drawer under the coffeepot." She angled around the couch and leaned on his arm as she sat down carefully. "Why am I stiff all over?"

"Because you got thrown around like a ragdoll today?" *Damn, it hurts to think about that.* He moved to the kitchen and shuffled through the contents of the drawer she indicated, locating both acetaminophen and ibuprofen. This was going to be a headache that could do with a little of each, so he opened both bottles and shook out the appropriate number of pills.

He pulled out his phone, checking to find an ***all clear*** from Tinder. His chest expanded hugely, stretching muscles still tense with fear as he breathed a sigh of relief. He knew there would no doubt be more debriefing to do later, but for now he could rest easy knowing Ella was safe.

My Ella.

Snagging a bottle of water from her fridge, Mad Dawg made his way back to the couch and sat next to her. "Here, baby." He held out the pills and unscrewed the top of the water, handing that to her as well.

"I should stretch. Do some yoga so I get out ahead of the soreness." She gulped the pills down with a couple of swallows and returned the bottle to him. "Thanks, Dawg."

"Why don't you rest first. Give your body that recovery time I keep hearing you talk about. No reason to push things. Let's hang out here on the couch and watch one of those romance movies you and Chicken like. I promise I don't hate them. I just wanna be here with you." *Need to be with her is more like it.* He set the closed bottle to the side, picked up the remote and dropped it in her lap. Grabbing a blanket from the back of the couch, he pulled her close and flipped it over them both. "This is comfy, yeah?"

She settled against his side and laughed softly, turning on the TV. "It is comfy. Just like our first date."

Her words made him smile. *Hell yeah we're dating. I like the sound of that.*

Chicken climbed on the couch on the other side of Ella, shoving at the blanket with his nose until he created a space for him to crawl underneath. "Dog thinks so, too." He stretched and ruffled Chicken's head. "Good boy."

On the TV, a show started playing and he kept most of his attention on Ella instead of looking away. Stroking the back of her head softly, he threaded his fingers through her hair, straightening it and gently unknotting a couple of tangles he found. It wasn't long before her breathing evened out, her body relaxing fully against him.

Mad Dawg kept up the tender touches, angling his head so he could see part of her face. Without more than that, he was content watching her sleep. *Keep her safe all her days, if she'll let me.*

When she eased back to wakefulness after a couple of hours, his back complained, but he didn't care.

Worth it.

She was tousled, warm and sweet, with her beautiful face showing a quiet pleasure at his presence.

He marked the moment when she remembered what had happened that morning, but any concern was fleeting, followed quickly by a deeper, knowing expression of affection.

"I feel better. You were right about the resting thing." She stretched an arm up, then angled herself across his lap, one hand propping up her head. "You are one comfy pillow, Dawg."

"And you're fuckin' gorgeous, Ella."

The smile she gave him was brilliant, shining with joy. It filled him with satisfaction, knowing she'd aimed it at him.

"You're not half bad yourself, mister."

"Hungry? Need anything? There's still some water here." He reached for the bottle, but her hand intercepted him, bringing his palm to her cheek.

She turned her head to press a kiss to his hand, then settled, looking at him. "I could eat." Her voice was low, quiet, private. "But what I'd like more than food is to feel like we're back to normal. Maybe make out with you a little."

He blinked slowly in surprise. "I can make that happen." Cradling the back of her head, he pulled her towards him as he leaned forward, their lips meeting for a tender moment. "Here, or?"

"Bedroom," she said without hesitation, pushing herself up a little. "Definitely need a door between us and Nuggie."

The dog's head popped out of the covers when she said his name, the lopsided puff between his ears lending the dog a comical look. He woofed quietly, then whined.

"See what you mean," Mad Dawg said with a chuckle. "Let's get you upright. I'll check in with my brothers quick, and then meet you in there."

"Thanks, that'll give me a minute to hit the necessary room." She folded in half and swung her legs over the side of the couch, palms to the floor, lifting her ass off the cushions. "Oh, man. That stretch is good." She gathered the blanket and rumpled it on the couch cushions, making a nest for the dog. "There you go, Nuggie. Be a good boy."

From the dog's betrayed expression, Mad Dawg wasn't sure he appreciated the gesture.

Ella disappeared down the hallway and he went to the kitchen, grabbing a fresh bottle of water as he looked at his phone. A quick text exchange later, he was reassured things would remain quiet. The entirety of the threat had been eliminated, according to Tinder.

Many thanks

He grinned when he got a thumbs-up in response. *Understated, as always.*

As he walked past the couch, the dog lifted his head, a grumpy glare directed towards Mad Dawg.

"I know," he said softly, ruffling the dog's ears. "Promise not to hog all her attention all the time. But tonight, I need this." Chicken whined, pressing his nose against Mad Dawg's hand. "Maybe more than she does, right." With one last tousle, he left the dog to his unhappy grump, grinning as the whine came again.

Turning into the bedroom, he stopped in surprise. Ella was already in bed, covers pulled up to her chin. Even swaddled as she was, he could see her shivering from here. He pulled the door closed behind him.

"Oh, honey," he crooned, divesting himself of his leathers and jeans. The socks were dropped at the bedside, and he crawled in beside her, wearing his tee and briefs. Reaching across to pull her closer, he was shocked to find her naked. Hot, bare skin formed an endless canvas underneath his wandering hands. "Sweetheart."

She curled against him, head to his shoulder, thigh thrown over his hips. He had to struggle not to thrust up against the warm pressure.

"Today was shit." The toneless quality of her voice along with the proclamation was frightening, and he wrapped his arm around her shoulders a little tighter. "Total, absolute shit."

"Yeah, it was. Scared the fuck out of me, them taking you like that. Not knowing if you were okay. Fucked with my head, Ella. Big time."

She stirred restlessly, cheek skimming across his chest. He felt the hot gust of her breath a moment before she pressed a kiss to the soft cotton. "Can you lose this, Dawg?" Her fingers plucked at the fabric. "I'd really like to feel you tonight. I need the contact. It'll ground me, I think. Make me less scattered to the wind."

He did a half crunch, hand reaching behind him to grab the shirt by the collar and drag it off. Settling back to the mattress, he pulled her against him again, then arranged the blanket around them. "Better?"

"Much," she whispered, her lips finding his skin this time in a gentle kiss. "So much better." Her palm glided down his belly, then back up. She trailed a touch through the hair on his chest, patting it down, then fluffing it again. "Everything about today was terrifying. Except one." Her voice tried to adopt the unmoved tone, but it shook a little this time. "The only thing good was seeing you. Knowing that I was right. I'd told myself over and over that you'd move heaven and earth to find me. I was right. That? That was good."

"Felt good getting my hands on you. Holding you in my arms." He traced the edge of the bruise on the side of her head with one finger. "Wish it hadn't happened at all. Hate like fuck you got hurt."

"Why did they come for me?" She scoffed and shook her head. "I know what they chattered on about, but they couldn't know for sure that you and I had a connection." Her hand hovered above his chest, fingers wavering. "Even if it's so solid I can nearly feel it here. They didn't have that certainty."

Mad Dawg pulled in a slow breath, letting the faith behind her words sink into his heart. *One in a million, right here in my arms.* "My boss in the club, the president of the whole shebang, he's got a theory he's pursuing right now." How much to tell her was in question, but he had to give her this much. *She's more than earned it.* "He thinks there was a member of my club who may have fed them info. I'll know more by tomorrow, but he's gonna plug that leak with prejudice." Tinder's text on the topic had been brief, but the anger and betrayal had burned through the few words. Those emotions were matched by his own. *Took my Ella.* Bending his neck, he kissed the crown of her head gently once, twice, a third time, reassuring himself she was here and safe. "I'm the one who put you at risk. By talking about how much I liked you, they took that info and ran with it."

"Well, at least it wasn't all done for a lie." Her response was mild, and he couldn't find any new tension in her body.

"Ella, did you hear me? It was my fault you got hurt." Twisting to his side, he faced her, their lips separated by a couple inches of smooth pillowcase. He hated the thought that the truth might drive her away, but the reality was clear in his mind. *She deserves to know.* "My fault."

"Nope. No siree. Do not take that on, my friend. It's their fault. Not yours. You didn't tell them 'oh hey, make sure you snag the chick that runs the yoga studio because you can leverage me then,' did you? No, you talked to people you trusted in a place you thought was safe about the feelings burgeoning for the chick that runs the yoga studio." He opened his mouth, but she didn't give him time to respond, just plowed ahead. "You aren't the asshole here. It's the guys who took... took... me. They took me." Her voice cracked. "Oh my goddess, Dawg, they *took* me."

She began to cry, eyes clenched shut. Covering her mouth with one hand, she pressed her face against his chest, trying to bury the sounds that escaped.

He didn't shush her, didn't try to soothe her. Rolling to his back, he pulled her against his side, holding her tightly.

This is the right time for this to come out now, where she's safe, and knows I'd protect her at all costs.

Her body shook with the force of the sobs, shoulders shuddering as she sucked in each breath with a struggle. Every cry was another fracture in his heart. *But this isn't about me.* His sentence was to witness as she came to grips with what had happened. *I'll hold her forever.* The wetness of her tears ran down his chest, disappearing into the sheet underneath, and still he held her quietly.

Minutes stretched out, and finally the racking sobs eased, trailing off with a series of hiccupping sounds. Her hands clutched at him, making sure he wasn't going to release her, not giving any room between them. He tightened his hold in response, finally making the first sounds of comfort.

"Shhhhhh, Ella. I've got you, beautiful." Her head shook, hair moving back and forth. "Yeah, I do. I'm here and not going anywhere."

"I—" Another sob escaped and her indrawn breath broke in a dozen places. "Dammit." The muttered curse vibrated from her lips to his skin, and he smiled. She pulled in another broken breath. "I'm a mess."

"No, you aren't." He half rolled to the side, reaching to the nightstand where he'd seen a box of tissues. Retrieved, he held them above her head. "Want some of these?" She shifted to look up, saw what he had, and nodded. He plucked a handful of tissues out, letting the box drop on the other side of Ella before offering them to her.

"Thanks," she whispered, and snuffled, blowing her nose noisily several times. When she pulled back and looked up at him again, it was with red eyes and nose, cheeks flushed from the crying. Her lips were thin and pale, the skin of her cheeks stretched taut with the residue of salty tears. "You're a damn good man, Dawg."

"I'm a biker." He shrugged, the covers drifting down a few inches. He ran his hand over her shoulder and down her back. "Not a good man."

"You've more morals and higher ethics than most people I know." She got in another good nose blow, rubbing it vigorously. "And that's saying something, because these days I try to only surround myself with people who bring good karma with them. Good vibes."

"Maybe we see things a little different in places, but I do the same. My brothers all follow the same creed as me, and that matters. It's a constant, you know? That knowledge is why it sucks to know one of them might have had a hand in what happened today." Smiling at her, he plucked the used tissues from her fingers and dropped them to the floor. "However, I can attest that you are goodness, through and through, Ella."

"I try," she said quietly, not brushing off his compliment. "That matters to me, too. We vibe in a good way, you know?"

"Yeah." He moved to kiss her and she lifted her chin, meeting him halfway. Their lips touched in a brief caress before he pulled back, staring into her eyes. There was heat there, a dancing desire he wanted to fan to flames. "I do know. We vibe well."

Her hand was pressed flat against his belly, fingers pointed down. She started to slide her palm across his skin, then laughed when she encountered his briefs.

"Lose them, please, sir." Hooking a thumb in the waistband, she started tugging them down his hip. Mad Dawg rolled to his back and shucked them off, then stayed put when she shifted to lay tightly against him. "Better," she said, dropping a smacking kiss to his shoulder. "I want you. Is that okay?" Her fingers curled around his cock, the shock of the touch nearly making him fold in half. His dick immediately chubbed up, blood rushing to his groin. His balls prickled with anticipation as she gave him a single, slow stroke. "Is this okay?"

"More than." He bit down on his bottom lip, mentally pulling up an engine's schematic as he tried to tamp down his body's reaction. Just the feel of her hand on him was enough to stretch his control. "But you better go slow."

"I can work with slow. I like slow way better than fast when it comes to pleasure." She spread out on her belly, upper body braced above his so her firm breasts trailed across his chest. Slipping lower in the bed, she traced a path down his body with her lips and tongue, turning her face to drag the unbruised side against him with a hum. When she reached his hips, she lavished the muscles and skin with kisses, wet and hot, her devilish tongue working against every inch she could reach.

Mad Dawg's hand settled on her shoulder, rubbing gently as she moved, not directing, just letting her do whatever she willed. He gave in to a groan when her breasts fell to either side of his rigid cock, her sternum rubbing along the length.

"Oh goodie, you don't hate this." She murmured the words with so much certainty he shouted a laugh.

"No, baby. I certainly do not hate what you've got goin' on." His hips shifted as he fought the urge to thrust against her. "Not one iota."

"Well, I kinda like it too." She shifted and her legs straddled one of his thighs, and the first touch of her drenched pussy nearly made him lose his mind. "Can you feel how much I like it?"

Her mouth came down on the head of his cock, tongue lapping and curling under the hood over the glans. She was still jacking him slowly, and he watched as the tip of her tongue disappeared behind the foreskin, all while lashing across the slit. He groaned and she pulled back to give the entirety of the length long, lascivious kisses, open-mouthed and wet.

He cocked his leg underneath her, shoving his heel against the mattress so she had a firm surface to push her pussy against. She started rocking, forward and back, her mouth sliding across his cock in time with her movements. Tiny moans filled the air, then she groaned, "Oh yes, please. That's very nice."

"Yeah, baby. Get yourself off like that. Just like that." His hand gripped her hair, slipping to the side as she bent her head to lap against his balls. The rough sac drew up tighter, and he clenched hard at the sensation that had his orgasm closer than ever. "Shit, Ella. I'm gonna go off before I get inside you, if you keep that up."

She shuddered and stilled, and he felt the pulsing of her pussy against his leg.

"Goddess, I nearly came myself right then at the thought. Dawg, I don't have condoms, but I'm on birth control." Her voice was strained, with an airless quality. She laughed softly and drew in a deep breath. "I'm good. Haven't had any partners in a long time, and I still test regularly. Shitty reasons, but I'm glad of the results right now. I'm down for it if you are."

"Taking you bare?" His head swam with the thought of nothing between them. "I've never done that. Not ever. And my tests are all good too. You sure, baby?"

"Oh, yeah," she groaned as she ground herself against his leg again. "So sure. Mega sure. Like take-me-now sure. Please."

He planted his other heel in the bed and flipped them. Ella let out a tiny shriek, then laughed again as he spread out on top of her. A quick roll of his hips had him dropping between her knees, and she angled her legs wide for him. Mad Dawg fell into the cradle of her hips, his cock pinned between their bodies.

"That was effective," she whispered, sounding out of breath. "I'm a big fan of efficiency, so points for that too. Yay."

"Wanted you under me for a long damn time. Since the first time I saw you through the window, all glowing and happy as you stretched and twisted. So fuckin' beautiful, inside and out." Mad Dawg pushed up on his arms, elbows locked so he hovered over her. They were connected from the waist down, but he wanted a long look at her like this. It felt momentous.

Because I'm building memories with her.

Hair a mess, spread out on the pillow like a seductive fan, her face had regained a tint of pink in her cheeks, and now her eyes were clear, staring up at him, any fear or sadness gone. A smile flickered across her lips as she wound one hand behind his neck. Not pulling him down, just touching, giving him this moment to study and look his fill. "You're even more gorgeous than I already knew." Her breasts were small, mounded on her chest. Taut muscles in her arm flexed as she held onto him. The tendons in her neck lent her a look of strength, but the expression on her face was soft, filled with affection. "Gonna love you, Elodie."

"Gonna let you, Dominick," she responded with a smile. Her tongue darted out, dampening her luscious lips. "You wanna get goin' on that sometime this century? A woman might think a man wasn't as ready as I can feel you are." She rolled her hips, moving her hot pussy against his dick.

He groaned as he dropped to one forearm, mouth hovering over hers as he reached between them to grasp his cock. Positioning himself at her opening, he held there a moment, then pressed in slowly. He entered her in pulses, pushing in and pulling out partway, then taking her deeper. Each slide built the pleasure, until he was buried balls deep and his belly was quivering with how hard it was to hold back.

"Feels so good. Fuck, Ella," he muttered, dipping down for a quick kiss.

Breathless, she chased his lips, demanding a deeper caress. She fell back to the pillow with a sigh, and nodded. "Yes, Dawg. Fuck. Fuck me." One hitch of her hips was all it took to break his uncertain control.

He dropped his forehead to hers, holding her gaze as he began to drive into her, the rhythm quickly settling into a hard and fast pace. He wouldn't be able to sustain this for long. *Just long enough.* "You feel so good, baby. Hot and wet, and you're takin' my cock just right. Perfect for me, baby. Fuckin' perfect."

"Fill me up, fill me." She threw a hand over her head, palm flat to the headboard as she shoved herself down onto his cock. "Give me everything, honey. Give it to me like you want. Take what you want. You're everything I need, right here."

Mad Dawg ignored light scratching at the door, keeping his focus on Ella's face.

Her mouth twisted in a moan, and she arched up, body colliding with his as they moved together. The slap of skin was loud.

"That's it, baby." He put his mouth to her ear, whispering, "Take yourself there."

"I won't leave you behind." Her panting cry came as tension filled as her body. "Oh, please. Please. Fill me." She tightened, writhing underneath him, her muscles taut as she lifted over the razor's edge of pleasure and fell into her orgasm. "Oh, Dawg. Please. Please." She wailed, "*Please.*"

"I got you, baby." He raked his teeth across the side of her throat, placing a series of hard, sucking kisses against her skin. His hips rose and fell, circling and rolling, dragging every ounce of enjoyment out of her. When she slowly began to relax underneath him, Mad Dawg unleashed himself, pounding hard and deep, bringing himself to the precipice within a handful of gasped breaths. Then he was coming, the overwhelming pressure pulsing through him as scorching heat surrounded the head of his cock. His spine stiffened, head drawing back in a sharp cry. The first spasm passed, and he curled himself around her, hips stuttering through another wave of passion.

A howl sounded from outside the bedroom door and Mad Dawg jolted, the movement making Ella catch her breath with a tiny exclamation. The dog cried out again, scratched at the door, and howled long and shockingly out of tune, like fingernails on a chalkboard.

Ella laughed, and the sound seemed to provoke Chicken, who responded with a series of wailing screams that could have been mistaken for a woman being killed. Or something being killed, anyway. *Maybe a chicken.*

Mad Dawg collapsed to the side, his cock slipping out as he laughed harder than he had in a long time. Laughter that would have seemed foreign only a few hours ago. *She's so fuckin' good for me.*

Ella spread herself over the top of him, still cackling madly, a hand settling on either side of his face. Staring into her eyes, he lay in amazed wonder as she choked out a returning howl, then followed her lead. His awkward attempts spun them off into greater hilarity, and the dog into another series of wailing cries.

When she bent close and kissed him, he took her laughter into his mouth, swallowing that joy, and made a promise to himself he would always make sure she had laughter in bed.

Always. My Ella.

***

Elodie

The sun woke her, streaming through the open curtains with unexpected intensity. It was late morning. *Shit. I've overslept.*

Elodie blinked several times, as waves of heat from the body next to her registered. *Larger than Chicken. And way cuter.* She grinned at the realization it was Dawg.

She turned to her side and propped on an elbow to gaze down at him. He was conventionally handsome, sharp cheekbones and a strong jawline covered with a short beard. His looks were one of the things that had initially flustered her around him. It had only been after she'd realized he either didn't know or didn't care about his looks that she'd dug deeper. Humility was apparently one of her turn-ons. *Who knew I liked them humble?* Through the months, their scant minutes-long conversations when their days overlapped hadn't done anything to change her opinion of him.

The experiences and situations over the past couple of days hadn't dented that opinion either.

"Gorgeous, sweet, kind, generous, filled with an exacting self-expectation that far exceeded what others might demand—you're a flippin' catch, Dawg."

"Not as much as you'd think," he muttered as he rolled in her direction, snuffling against her breasts as she rested a hand on his head. "You're warm."

"And you're like a furnace. Burned hot all night." She grabbed a handful of hair and tugged gently. "Not that I'm complaining, mind you. I don't hate that. I'll save money on electricity with you in my bed."

"Glad it's a point in my favor." His lips moved against her skin, and she shivered with delight as he pressed gentle kisses across the slope of her breasts. "I like the idea. Plus, there's lots of perks of you being in bed with me too." Taking one peak into his mouth, he sucked deep, the delicious sensation causing Elodie's back to arch as she pulled him closer with the handhold she had on his hair. "That's one perk." His murmur was muffled as he moved to the other breast, lavishing the same attention there. "And lookie what I found. I see there's another."

"Well, those perks appreciate your attention." She bent her neck, pressing a kiss against the side of his head. "Love it, actually."

"Good," he told her, pulling back enough to look up at her. "That's the desired reaction, lady." He shifted around, pushing up farther in the bed, so they were face-to-face in mirroring positions with heads propped on hands. His gaze traveled across her face, coming to rest exactly where it still ached a little. "How you doin' this mornin'?"

"I'm good." He made a sound in his throat, and she pressed a hand against his bare chest. The thudding of his heart slammed against her palm, and she smiled, understanding where he was coming from. *Maybe there's the tiniest bit of fear there.* "No, really," she reassured him. "I'm good. Will memories of the events jump up and bite me in the ass at some point? Maybe. But maybe not. Remember I trusted you'd come for me. That makes it less scary to think about. My certainty helped get me through then, and will in the future, too." Shaking her head, she leaned close enough to touch his lips with hers. Dawg stared into her eyes as she pulled back. "When—*if* the ass-biting happens, we can deal with it."

"That easy?" He lifted his hand to trace along her jaw and throat, warm fingers cupping around the back of her neck. He kneaded her flesh gently, with the smallest tug in his direction. "Really?"

"Really." She moved with his unspoken request, sliding closer to him in the bed. "It's that easy."

He brought his mouth to hers in a brief kiss, pulling her body towards him as he rocked her to her back. Dawg loomed over her, bright and questioning eyes darting across her features, watching everything. She gave him back only peace and contentment, pushing it through her mind so it would flow into her face. It wasn't a façade, and she hoped he'd understand. Then the lines on his face relaxed slightly, as the corners of his mouth turned up.

I knew he'd get it. We just vibe.

"Okay," he said gently, his lips touching down for an instant, the caress quick and tender. "Okay," he repeated, the smile now dancing in his eyes. "In that case, prepare yourself, woman."

She spread her legs and stretched her arms high overhead, glad she hadn't donned any clothing after their rounds of sex during the night. Each muscle came to life at her direction, tensing then relaxing until she puddled on the mattress. "I'm ready, Dominick."

"Meant to tell you last night. I kinda like that, Ella." He shifted to cover her, his hips sliding naturally into the vee created by her thighs. "My name on your tongue."

"You'd like something else on my tongue better." She laughed softly as his eyes darkened. "Oh ho, someone likes that idea."

"I think I'd like absolutely anything with you." Dawg's tone had gone somber, as if this proclamation needed gravity. "Everything, Ella. As long as it's with you, that's all I want."

Butterflies took up residence in her belly at his confession. *Same page, honey.* There was nothing she wanted more than everything with him.

"Sounds like a lot more than a roll in the hay. That's weightier. More robust. Longer. Deeper." She kept her gaze locked with him. Hoping he knew how serious she was taking this conversation. "I kinda like hearing that."

"Yeah." He blew out a careful breath, the air touching her face as she reached to lace her fingers behind his head, pulling him closer. They shared breaths for a few moments, staring at the other. "I'm talkin' about a fuckton more than a hookup. I've had a crush on you forever, but that's changed now."

"Changed how? Also, a crush?" She crooked an eyebrow at him, ignoring the twinge of pain it caused. "How did I miss that when I had the same on you?" She touched her lips to his, and he immediately took control of the kiss, bending his neck to deepen the caress. His tongue begged for entrance and she granted the gentle request, opening eagerly for the sweet connection. When he pulled back finally, she blinked slowly up at him. "You make me drunk, Dominick."

"Changed for the better, as far as I'm concerned. And as far as gettin' you kiss-drunk off a single kiss, I think that's on the pro side of the chart too. Definitely a perk.

Anything I can do to please you, that's gonna be my mission." He shifted, rolled his hips, and groaned far back in his throat. "Jesus, baby. You fit against me just right."

His erection was rigid between them, pressing firmly against her clit. She reached down and cupped her fingers around the shaft, lifting her hips to bring the head to her core.

"You ready for me, Ella?" He gave a tentative thrust so the glans parted her entrance, and it slid easily through the wetness there. "Fuck me," he whispered, bending his head to bury his face against her throat. "Jesus, baby. You're always ready for me."

"Something about you does it for me, Dom." She skated her hands up and down his back, pushing the covers down so she had unfettered access. Grabbing one ass cheek in each hand, she pulled him tight against her, lifting her hips at the same time so he slipped deep inside with a single push. "There," she moaned softly.

"There," he groaned his approval. "Right fuckin' there, Ella."

"Fuckin' move," she told him, imitating his voice and startling him into a laugh that caused delicious shivers inside her. "Need you to fuckin' move right now, Dawg."

"Your wish is my command, baby."

The rest of the morning was spent in bed, broken only by quick trips to the bathroom and kitchen, to clean up and find food and coffee.

And deal with a largely disgruntled canine.

Chapter Eight

Elodie

"So, he wants something long-term. That shouldn't be a big deal, right?"

Chicken lifted his head to look at her over the arm of the couch, and grumped.

Elodie laughed as she ran the dust cloth across the tops of the door frames a final time. She'd been busily cleaning for hours, her unsettled thoughts needing an occupied body to be able rise to the top of her consciousness. She'd tried a long yoga session earlier, attacking some of the complicated poses which left her with aching muscles, but her brain had still been mush.

"I like him. I don't see why my head is afraid of that fact."

She grimaced at Chicken.

"Okay, that's a lie. I do know." She folded her legs to sit on the floor and immediately had a lap full of dog. "It's scary, thinking about going down that road. Again." He licked the side of her face, sniffing at the fading bruising. "You understand. I knew you would, Nuggie. I need to tell him all about my past. He needs to know."

It was the second day she'd kept the yoga studio closed, not willing to reopen just yet. Dom had offered for her to ride in with him this morning, but she'd begged off. Returning to the studio was inevitable, but the thought of it had the ass-biting happening she'd referred to the first night.

"Maybe I need to just go in on my own." She rumpled Chicken's topknot, ruffling his ears. "I think that's it. I don't want an audience watching to see if I'll fall apart. The expectation would bother me." Shoulders straight, she grounded her seat bones and drew in a deep breath. "I won't react badly. It's my space, and it's up to me to make it safe again."

Shooing Chicken off her lap, she stood and looked down at her leggings and shirt.

"Entirely appropriate. No need to delay." Hooking a leash on Chicken's collar, she followed his dancing path to the door. "Afterwards, we'll celebrate." She grabbed her purse and slung it over her shoulder, hand on the doorknob. "With nuggies for my Nuggie."

Parking behind the studio, she carefully closed her car door, not wanting to draw Dom's attention just yet. Unlocking the back door had her hands moving with muscle memory, even as Chicken tangled her legs with the leash. She laughed quietly as they nearly fell through the doorway, the dog excited at being allowed in a new place. It was the work of moments to kill the alarm with the new code Dom had given her, and then she leaned against the shut and locked door, pressing both shoulders against the steel.

Chicken raced around the room, stopping every few feet to smell and nudge things with his nose. He was comfortable, easily accepting of the space, and Elodie's muscles slowly relaxed.

She made her way to the music pod and booted it up, putting a gentle playlist on to fill the room with soothing sounds. Mats were scattered here and there, a reminder that she hadn't been able to clean up after her last class.

Happy to have something to do, she picked them up and sanitized them, folding them over the rail running along the walls. Chicken followed her every step, staying close to her now she was moving around. He found a block and tried to nudge it towards her with his nose, growling low when it went in unexpected directions.

Elodie laughed at his antics, stopping abruptly when a brief knock came from the back door.

"Who is it?" This hesitation wasn't something she'd never felt before, and it grated on her that even this carried a tiny bit of fear.

"Mad Dawg. It's me, baby."

Thumbing the deadbolt, she opened the door and drew it open. Dom stood in the doorway, his gaze locked on her. His face carried an expression of worry, brows bunched over narrowed eyes. There was a flash at the corner of her eye and Elodie stomped on Chicken's leash just as he arrowed for the escape path, pulling him to an abrupt stop in front of Dom. The pooch immediately turned his attention to the man, leaping and bounding.

"Can I come in?" he asked, reaching down to ruffle Chicken's head.

"Oh, yeah." She stepped to the side, closing the door behind them and locking it again. "Sorry. Lost my manners there for a minute. Struck dumb by your handsome face."

"Baby," he murmured, sweeping his arms around her. Elodie went willingly, nestling against his shoulder with a sigh. "I didn't think you were coming in, but then heard the music. Wanted to make sure it was really you."

"It's really me." She wrapped her arms around his waist, holding tightly. "I'm glad you came to check on me. Isn't that silly?" Laughing softly, she angled her head to look into his face. "I was making myself crazy back at home. There's only so much cleaning one person can do before going insane, and I was nearing the limit."

"I'd have come and got you. Or met you out back." He caressed the curve of her cheek, fingers trailing along the edges of the waning bruising. His brows furrowed deeply again as his gaze followed the touch of his hand against her face.

Elodie suspected he would continue to be protective long after the physical evidence of her kidnapping faded away.

I'm okay with that. I kinda like him going all caveman. Me Ella, Dom mine.

"Don't be mad, but I think I needed to do this on my own. I'm very glad you're here now, if that helps with the sting." She was rewarded by a small smile, and his hand wrapped around the back of her neck, pulling her up for a kiss. "Oh, goodie," she murmured against his mouth. "One of my favorite things."

"What's that?" He trailed kisses along her neck, teeth dropping gentle nips, while his tongue darted out to soothe the skin. "Your favorite things?"

"Your mouth on my mouth." She gasped and leaned into his body, letting him take her weight. "Love that." Pulling back, she placed a palm against his chest. "But we're in my workplace, which means it's a nookie-free zone."

"Damn, I didn't know I was violating some rule here." His mouth didn't slow, continuing to tease along the column of her throat. "I'm a rule breaker, baby. You gotta know that up front." Each word was accompanied by a gust of hot air across tongue-dampened skin, and she shivered. "That's a good reaction. Tells me you're up for some rule breakin' too."

"Dom," she breathed his name, shivering in his hold. "We need to talk."

He froze in her arms, and she played back her words.

"Oh shit, not that way." Elodie pulled back, lifting his chin with her fingers. "It's a good talk, I promise. Well, I think it's good. See…" She winced at the hurt and bewildered expression on his face. "No, it's good. I just need to tell you about me. My past. I don't want you to be blindsided by anything."

"You kill someone?" His eyes darkened, mouth twisting. "Kick puppies? Laugh at disabled people?"

"What? No. Why would you think that?" Pausing for a breath, she steadied herself. "This is what happens when I try to start in the middle of a mental conversation. I'm so sorry, Dom. I didn't mean to upset you."

"If you did any of that, we'll talk. If you haven't, and those are some of the worst things I can think of on the fly, then I doubt what you tell me will have any sway in how I feel about you." His expression softened. "But I promise to listen. Whatever it is, I'll listen."

"That's all I can ask," she said, rising to her toes to brush her lips against his. "How about we do this tonight, so there's no waiting and angsting?" She kissed him again. "All of that would be completely on my side. I already know you don't do angst."

"Life's too short." He gave her a smile, but it didn't reach his eyes. "Tonight sounds good. I was comin' over anyway."

"I was hoping." Chicken reared up on her leg, bumping her elbow. "So was Nuggie, seems like. I'll make dinner and we can chat over food." Nerves wound through her belly. "Fair warning to you. It's a hard topic for me. Hard as in difficult to put into words. I don't like even thinking about that time in my life."

"Then I'll hold your hand or hold you. Whatever you need, Ella." This time his smile lifted the corners of his eyes, and when his hand landed in the small of her back, it was to urge her closer. "No rule breakin' today. But would it be okay if I hung out with you for a bit? I've got a couple hours before it's time to open the shop."

"I'm going to do yoga," she warned. "That's not a spectator sport."

"Long as you take it easy on me, I'd be down for some stretching." Leaning in, he kissed her lips quickly, ending with a smack. "Lemme lose the boots and socks, and I'll be ready."

"I'll say it again, Dom. You're a good man." The last of her tension fled, and she shook out her arms and hands to release the tingling sensation. "I'll get some mats ready for us and we'll do this thing."

She shook out a couple of towels to the side and made a nest for Chicken, who immediately took up residence, turning in a tight circle several times to show his approval.

Then she put down mats, doubling the one for Dom. Looking up, she watched as he removed his vest and folded it tidily before setting it on top of his boots. His wallet already lay to the side. He glanced in her direction and their gazes met and caught, the sensation that he could see deep inside her filling her up with wonder.

He's the one.

Aloud, she said, "Shall we begin?" Indicating his mat, she folded her legs and settled into an easy pose. "Let's start with breathing." He'd told her about using box breathing while looking for her, and she knew he'd make the connection too. "It's a great grounding effort."

"Yeah it is." He was a little less clumsy getting to the mat, and she grinned. "Yeah, yeah, get your yucks out. I might have been trying to practice a little."

"That's good. After all, yoga *is* a practice." Closing her eyes, Elodie demonstrated the breathing technique, counting softly. "One, two, three, four, hold."

Within a couple minutes, the atmosphere in the studio was calmer, easier, and Elodie was well centered. She opened her eyes to find Dom dutifully breathing slowly, his shoulders angled away from his ears, palms flat on his thighs. She stared at him. As when he was sleeping, the relaxed lines of his face accentuated the handsome features.

"Oh goddess, I'm a lucky lady," she whispered, and met his gaze when his eyes snapped open. "Let's move to cat/cow breathing. Knees hip width, hands shoulder width, and we breathe in as we drop our belly to the ground in cow, lifting heart center to the sky."

He adopted the new pose without argument, following her lead in a way that gratified far more than any class ever had.

"Now roll the back up, feeling every vertebra fall into place as we arch the pelvis, breathing out stress and ill will. Head down between our shoulders, this is a way to stretch out the back, releasing tension. And back to cow, lifting heart center to the sky as we breathe in deeply."

The next thirty minutes went the same way, and as they came to an end of their shared practice, Elodie smiled when she felt Dom's hand brush hers, fingers twining together. They lay on their backs, breathing slowly.

"Good boy," she crooned and Dom laughed.

"Thanks, I think." He laughed again.

"Not you. That goes without saying." She smiled without opening her eyes. "But, Chicken was really good at waiting. Okay, go."

The dog's first jump landed him in Dom's stomach, eliciting a loud "oof" in response. His second had him snuggled along her side, feet aimed at Dom, licking both of their faces wildly as he kicked and wiggled.

"Oh, yeah." Dom groaned, clutching his belly dramatically as he chuckled. "He's a real good boy."

Now or never.

Her stomach rolled. The things she needed to tell him would be hard to get through. But understanding the past was critical to creating a future. *Got that universe? I want to create a future with this man. Please, and thank you.*

"Dinner when you close the shop? You'll still come over, right?"

His fingers gave hers a squeeze. "Absolutely" was his immediate response. "Always and any time. Any time at all."

"Good." She wondered if he could feel her palm sweating. "Real talk, I'm nervous about telling you some of my—history."

"Already told you the deal breakers for me. And baby, you don't have to do anything you aren't ready for, Ella. I like who you are, and as you'd put it, I like the vibe between us. It's real and honest, and I really like that."

"I think it's something I need to do, Dom."

"Then we will. But you don't have to feel like you're alone. I'm an open book, and I'll answer any questions you have for me. Anything." He patted Chicken, who wiggled wildly in ecstasy. "I'll be at your place. Don't be surprised if I close early."

Elodie laughed softly and pushed up to one elbow, looking down at his face. She traced his brows with a fingertip, then bent close for a soft kiss, a connection between them that started with their mouths and grew by leaps and bounds. Hand on his chest, she could count each quick beat of his heart, thudding in sync with her own.

"I'll see you then." Looking around the studio, she took in a heavy breath and held it for a count of four before blowing it out. "And thank you for helping me take back this space. I was worried about coming here. Worried how it'd feel. And it was scary."

"I'd think it was more weird if it wasn't frightening. Something terrible happened here, an invasion of your sense of safety. I expect there will still be times when it's got a sense of something off." He reached up, fingers tucking a strand of hair behind her ear. "I'm gonna be here any time you want me. We can put in an intercom if you want, make it easier for you to check in that you've got backup."

"There are some dark emotions here, for sure." Elodie looked left to right, studying the angles the mirrors gave to innocent objects like the rolling tray she kept for the yoga blocks. "I think I'll smudge the place. Help cleanse it before I reopen Monday." Leaning her cheek into his touch, she looked down again to find Dom staring at her. "I've already posted on social media that I'll be back. Can't disappoint those serenity seekers."

"Yoga makes you happy. I think it would be good for you to continue to share that with your class members. Just look at you now. Half an hour coaching me, and you're glowing and settled." His palm cupped her throat, thumb pressing in on her pulse for a moment. "You're way steadier than me. But I think this helped me, too."

"I'm glad. It's not a panacea for everything, but it can help with a lot."

He pushed up to a seated position, fingers absently ruffling Chicken's fur. "I should get off the floor before I can't."

Elodie smiled at him, feeling the stretch of her lips as the pleasure painted her face. "Can't have that. Let's get you up, then." She unfolded gracefully, planting her feet wide as she reached down a hand. "Come on, you. Up, up."

He took the offered help with a smile, coming to his feet a little slower. Once upright, he didn't stop moving, but leaned into her and dragged Elodie into an embrace. Her arms wrapped around his upper back and neck, and she held on tightly as he did the same.

"I'm glad I met you, lady." His words were muttered softly against her neck, each movement of his lips causing a ripple of gooseflesh to rise on her arms. "Real fuckin' glad."

"Me too." Her murmur was eclipsed by Chicken's rising whine, and when she glanced down, his mismatched eyes were dancing with doggie humor. "Nuggie agrees, I think."

"Thank God. I'd hate to hear what he'd have to say if he didn't approve."

She started laughing, clinging to Dom's shoulders to hold herself upright.

His lips on hers silenced the sound but didn't take away the sense of rightness and pleasure she felt in his arms.

***

Mad Dawg

From the few hints Ella had dropped earlier, Mad Dawg assumed the talk she felt compelled to have would be about an ex. Whether that was husband or boyfriend didn't matter. As long as the *ex* part of the equation was no longer in the picture.

Don't matter. She's mine and we both know it.

As he'd promised, he'd closed the shop nearly three hours early, just so he could be here with her. When he rolled to a stop in front of her house, he'd already planned and discarded a dozen ideas to make this easier on her. It was causing her so much anxiety that he just wanted it over, whatever it was.

He pulled out his phone and glanced at the screen. There was a message from Rocker, so he unlocked the device, navigating to the message app. The text was brief, just asking for a call later tonight. Mad Dawg heard a sound and looked up in time to see the door swing wide, Ella and Chicken framed in the doorway. Making a mental note to call his brother back, he locked the phone and shoved it deep in his pocket, moving around the bike and up the sidewalk.

Ella met him with open arms, wrapping herself around him so there wasn't room for a whisper between them. She held him tight, and he stroked up and down her sides and back, soothing her.

"I didn't know how much longer you'd be." She pulled back, linking their fingers together as she drew him into the house. "I've got a casserole ready to pop into the oven. Once I do, it'll be just less than an hour before we eat. Is that okay?"

"That sounds perfect," he assured her, moving with her easily. Chicken beat them to the couch, paws hanging over the back as he watched them approach. "Who's a good dog?" Chicken's tongue lolled out, his bright eyes wide as he wiggled in place. "What'd you do this afternoon?" Surprised when Elodie didn't pause at the couch, he kept pace with her into the bedroom.

Once the door was closed, she dropped his hand but didn't speak, just stared at the bed.

"Baby?" He came up behind her, propping his chin on her shoulder, arms around her waist. "What's going on in that head of yours?"

"I've got my shit together, you know?"

Puzzled by the odd opening, he nodded, strands of her hair catching in his beard. "Yeah, I do know. You're a business owner who's damn successful, have a great home, and a crazy dog. Doin' pretty damn well, if you ask me."

"Wasn't always the case." She twisted and he released his hold enough to let her turn in his arms, facing him. "My folks are old time hippies. Guess you can figure that out by my name. They didn't instill any good habits in me, mostly because they didn't have any themselves. I'm pretty sure my dad is my dad, but they were into doing what felt good, no matter who might get hurt." She pulled in a hard breath. "My ex-husband was part of their group, and at first it was okay." She shrugged. "Everything was not great, but okay. Then he wanted to leave the group, so I packed up and followed him."

"Hold up a minute and let's get comfortable, baby."

Mad Dawg steered her to the bed as he spoke and Ella went easily with him, knee-walking her way to the headboard to sit beside him. He kicked off his boots, leaving them to thump to the floor. Reaching out, he dragged her into his lap, pulling her close so she was leaning against him.

"How's that?"

"Better," she admitted, her next deep breath sounding like it came easier.

"I agree. Much better. Why'd your old man want to leave where your parents were?"

"Now I get it, you know? It was to isolate me. Sure, now I know, but let me tell you, it took a lot of therapy to get to that realization, because I didn't understand back at the time. I thought he loved me so much he wanted me all to himself. So I let it happen. First from my parents, and then everyone I knew. After that it was me not working, not having a job or my own money, because he 'wanted to take care of me' he said." She used air quotes around the words. "But then, things twisted. I was home all day, because he didn't like it when I went out. Even to the park or library. My place was at home."

"That's fucked up."

"Yeah, like I said I know better now. Should have listened to my bad vibes, you know? They were tingling and singing, but I ignored them. He loved me. He said he did. So much changed from the first date to when I left. I went through a terrible evolution. Because, the thing is, if you hear bad things about yourself often enough and loud enough, punctuated with beatings and fights, it becomes your truth."

Mad Dawg forced himself to keep breathing, not letting his arms tense around her. "Beatings?"

"Figured you'd latch onto that." She laughed, the sound raw with bitterness. "Yeah, one form of ensuring I understood my place. So, long story short, I got away from him and tried to go back to the commune, but my parents had moved on. Places like that don't have forwarding addresses, so I was out of luck finding them. It wasn't the same without them there, and once Dwight realized where I'd gone, he followed. So I left."

"Dwight's the ex?" A deep, simmering anger filled him. She might have kept the tale to the minimum, likely to spare him from the details, but he'd be damned if she'd go without justice. *Not on my fuckin' watch.* "Where's he now?" *I bet Denver could find him based on this info alone.*

"I know what you're doing." Ella tipped her head back, eyes angled up to meet his. "It's in the past, Dom. Well and proper, in the past. I found a job, then a good attorney. Divorced him, left his name in the dust, and took my maiden back. Forrester is mine, not his."

"See, I don't believe you. Not really. Not if the idea of telling me this has had you so worked up, Ella. Worked up for days. That doesn't say past to me." He wished it was behind her, but the way she'd trembled as she avoided talking in detail about the physical abuse was loud and clear.

"I wasn't worried about telling you." She wrinkled her nose. "Okay, lie. Sorry universe. Sorrier to you, Dom. Yes, I was worried, but more about what you'd think it said about me."

"What it says about you is you are a goddamned survivor. A strong fucking person in your own right, with value and purpose. You're a winner, thriving all the way around. Doesn't matter how far down the motherfucker tried to drag you, there was a path back up and you found it, and recovered yourself in the process. It tells me you're precious, because you've seen the worst in people, and come out the other end still letting a fuckin' biker like me get close. You trust your gut, and trust people, which means he never broke you." Her eyes filled with tears and Mad Dawg's throat closed, his words coming out rough, yet tender. "Found yourself, and then you found me. Now I'm the one that's the winner."

"Such a good man," she whispered. Clearing her throat, she said, "I did lose myself for a while. Credit wasn't something I understood. There was so much I had to learn." She shook her head, then leaned heavily on his shoulder. "I knew what I wanted to do, but it was years before I'd even let myself dream of having my own studio."

"What all kinds of work have you done? Things you didn't hate, I mean." He settled more comfortably against the headboard, crossing his legs at the ankle. "I bet you've got some stories."

"I do. On the hate side of the column is retail and food service." She shivered dramatically. "People don't see those workers as necessary, or providing a service, so they're mostly jerks to anyone behind a counter. Oddly enough, I enjoyed working at a bank the most. I didn't have to interface with people, just was backend accounting data entry. It's a far cry from the satisfaction I get from helping someone on their enlightenment journey, but it didn't suck. Still, it was just a job."

"Hmm. You, making order out of chaos. Yeah, I can see that." Leaning his head back, he smiled as she wiggled on his lap. "Careful, girlie, you might stir up some trouble if you keep that up."

Ella giggled, the sound light and sweet. "Tell me something about you that I don't know. Which is a lot, now that I think of it."

"Well, my history is tied up in the military and the club. Nothing really in between. I spent fifteen years in uniform, got out, found my brothers." He shrugged. "Never looked back."

"No relationships to speak of?" She arched away, staring up with a frown. "That doesn't compute, sir. You're too damn good-looking to not have an old girlfriend at least."

"Not since high school, and it wasn't anything serious. When she wanted to talk about going to college together, I broke it off. She wasn't right for me." He tightened his arms and dipped his chin to capture her mouth in a quick kiss. "No one has been right for me." He kissed her again. "Not until now."

"Hey." She laughed the word against his mouth. "This is new for both of us then, right? My first good relationship, and your first ever." Her hand slipped around the back of his neck, pulling him close again. "We'll teach each other the right way to do things."

"Sounds like a plan." He moved them down the mattress, until she was stretched out beside him. "Now that we've got those worrisome talks over and done with, I've got another plan in mind."

"Oh, do tell, Dom. What's on your mind."

His thumb grazed over her nipple, fingers curling around the swell of flesh. "I've got a lot on my mind, darlin'." Kissing her slowly, she groaned into his mouth when he parted her lips with his tongue, dipping and tangling with hers. "And it all starts now."

He shifted down her body, replacing his thumb with his mouth, sucking at the peaked flesh through the thin fabric, leaving it wet and molded to her body when he drew away. He pushed gently at her shoulder, and she went to her back, arms over her head, arching into his touch as he moved his attention to the other breast.

"Take it off," she urged, fingers fumbling with the hem of her shirt. "Please, Dom."

Kneeling between her thighs, he helped remove the strappy yoga shirt, then did the same with the form-fitting bra underneath. Spanning her waist with his hands, Mad Dawg let his fingers explore her sides and belly, stroking his thumbs slowly across the sleek swells of her hip bones. Hooking a finger in the waistband of her leggings, he tugged them down her legs, taking her underwear with as he finished undressing her.

Hovering over her completely clothed while she was naked felt decadent, as maddening as the rush of bliss that filled his chest. She'd bared herself to him tonight, told him all her secrets, and now was giving him her body. Her pleasure was in his hands, and he vowed not to disappoint her. *Never.*

Bending to trace a path across her chest with his mouth, he relished the resulting goose bumps that rose in the wake of his wandering tongue.

"Dom, everything you do feels so good." Her head went back on a moan when he shifted between her legs, lowering his groin to press the rough fabric of his jeans against her core. "Oh, goddess. Please."

"Tell me what you need, darlin'." Propping himself up with one bent arm, he used the other hand to push between her thighs. His thumb pulsed against her budded clit, dragging a gasp from her throat as she drew herself up in a crunch, mouth seeking his desperately.

"Everything you're doing. That's what I want." Her hands pushed at his shirt and waistband. "And naked, I need you naked. That's what I need, honey. Please."

The endearment built a ball of growing hunger deep in his belly. Even more than hearing his name on her lips, it was tied up in the way she'd spoken, voice full of desire, and a bone-deep trust that he'd do anything for her. He'd learned her, sure, but she knew him too. *Made for me.*

"I got you." Shifting back, he plucked one of her hands and draped it across her pussy. "Keep going. Wanna watch you while I get ready."

On his command, her fingers slipped through the soft folds, fingers shifting firmly side to side across the flesh of her mons. Her other hand rose to her breast, then traveled farther, tracing along the column of her throat in a touch that was light and delicate. A dichotomy of caresses he wanted the test of his life to memorize.

Dick stone hard behind the zipper it was trying to break through, he rushed through undressing, flinging everything except the vest hither and yon. Stumbling over his discarded boots in his hurry, he placed the folded vest on the dresser and turned back just in time to watch her legs move restlessly.

"Want you, baby." Stalking towards the bed, he placed a knee between her feet. Taking an ankle in each hand, he moved them to the sides, opening her wider. "So fuckin' hot, watching you play with yourself."

As if his words urged her on, her other hand joined the first, spreading her lips to show him two fingers plunging inside her pussy.

"Like what you see, big man?" The teasing note in her voice was followed by a breathy moan. "This is what I want from you. Inside me. Deep. Throbbing. Hard as you take me."

In response, he moved so he blanketed her, grabbing her wrists in his hands. One at a time he brought them to his mouth, watching as her eyes widened when he drew his tongue over each finger, dipping in between to ensure he didn't miss a drop of her taste.

His rigid cock nestled against her, and as he rolled his hips, the head notched into place. Another push and he was halfway inside, the slippery path even more evidence of her pleasure. He had to stop short of another thrust, though, cock pulsing as his balls drew tight against his body.

"Shit. Fuck, baby." He groaned as she clenched around him, her pussy trying to draw him deeper. "Hold on, give me a minute. So hot and tight, fuckin' fit me like a glove. Made for me." He buried his face against her neck, placing a sucking kiss where her throat joined her shoulder. "Gonna make you feel so good."

"Gotta move to do that, honey." Ella lifted her hips, giving him another tiny gasp and a moan. "Please. Move. Please." Her hands slid up and down his back, then traveled lower to cup his ass and pull him against her. Legs wrapped around his waist, she fucked herself on his cock for a span of breaths, then pulled back with a short laugh and slapped his ass cheek.

"Shit." The slight sting had him punching into her, cock bottoming out. He could feel the bristly hair of her pussy around the base of his shaft, his balls resting against the soft swell of her ass. "Woman, that's gonna get you a pounding."

"I'll take it over stillness." Her laughter was thin and airy, the timbre of her voice cracking. "Need you, Dom. Need you, honey."

"I've got you." He pushed up on braced arms, looking down the length of her body to where they were joined. "Had to get myself under control first, though. You feel so good, baby." He circled his hips as she bowed her back, the contact emphasized by the deep groan she gave at the movement. "So fuckin' good."

Her hands on his shoulders urged him down, so he lowered himself, propped on both elbows as he cradled her face in his hands. Slow, deep kisses followed; every tongue-tangling caress accompanied by a thrust of his hips until he found a rhythm that brought her higher. He slipped lower, and she tightened her legs around him, the position making his balls draw tight again.

"Dom, I'm there." Ella broke the kiss, head thrown back as she cried out. "Oh, please."

He nipped the tendons on her throat, picking up speed as his own orgasm barreled down the pike, hard and fast. Hips stuttering as he tried to draw out her pleasure, he grew still, cock throbbing demandingly where he was buried inside her. Resting his forehead between her breasts, he managed a couple more thrusts, drawing another cry from deep in her chest. Then he was gone, pushed over the edge by the tight, pulsing grip of her pussy. Coming deep inside her, filling her with his spend, the heat volcanic around the head of his cock.

When she drew her palms up his back he shuddered against her. Turning his head, he placed his ear against her chest, listening to the pounding of her heart. Mad Dawg stayed there for a long time, as their pulses slowed, sweat-slickened skin chilling in the open air. Her hands cradled his head, fingers stroking gently, slipping through the strands of his hair.

They stayed like that until he softened and slipped out of her, drawing a groan and a laugh from both of them.

He retrieved a damp cloth from the bathroom and cleaned them both up, then crawled into bed beside her. Flicking the covers over them, Mad Dawg curled himself behind her, slotting his knees into place tucked against hers.

With their fingers joined over her breast, he cradled her to him until they both fell asleep.

Chapter Nine

Mad Dawg

Standing behind the bar at the clubhouse, Mad Dawg loaded up the surface with beers drawn from the cooler underneath. Service to the club didn't stop when any of the members put the full club patch on their back. This was just one way he could give back to his brothers.

Tinder leaned his arms on the edge of the bar, reaching for one of the opened bottles. "Thanks, my brother." He tipped the bottle Mad Dawg's direction, then lifted it and took a long drink. "Good to see you, man. Glad everything's cool."

"Is it? Cool? Are they going to be a problem again?" He couldn't stop the questions, because while he'd been reassured via text over the days since Ella's kidnapping went down, no one would give him direct answers to what he wanted to know.

"Hold it for the meeting, brother. You know we've got your back, and that means we've got the back of your lady, too." Tinder tsked. "Won't let anything happen to her, ever again. Should know that."

"I do." He opened another few beers, then left his post, circling around the end of the bar so he could pull Tinder into a one-armed clinch. "I do, Prez, but damn, would it hurt you to let a man know what happened in detail?"

"Did you ever think maybe the detail wasn't for everyone to know?" Tinder pulled away and took another deep drink. "And keep it for the meeting, when we've got a handle on who's in the loop."

"Okay, okay." He grumbled his agreement. "It's just been fuckin' with my head."

Since the night he and Ella had talked through her past, Mad Dawg hadn't been able to shake the feeling another shoe was about to drop. Something in the air, maybe, but as she'd said more than once, like her, he liked to follow his gut. There'd been nothing on the security videos, because while Denver had reviewed each of them, so had Mad Dawg. *Just to be sure nothing was missed.* Not that he thought his brothers would do anything intentionally, but they didn't have a dog in the hunt like he did.

"Well, the news I have should unfuck your head pretty good." Tinder lifted a hand to his mouth and whistled around two fingers. "Hangarounds and prospects, you're dismissed. Be back next weekend, but in the meantime, vamoose."

"Mad Dawg." He turned to see Rocker walking his direction. "Well met, brother."

Pulling in Rocker for a back-pounding hug, he sighed. "Well met, man. Good to see you."

"Tinder tell you the news yet?" Mad Dawg pushed back to stare at him. "Guess not. Come on. This oughta be good."

"Be good?" Mad Dawg moved when Rocker shoved at his shoulder, preceding him into the meeting room. "What does that mean? Last time you found something amusing, I wound up with a patch I never expected."

"That was good too. Stop your whining. Baby." Rocker pulled a chair away from the table, spinning it and sitting with his arms folded on the back of the chair. "Big ole baby."

"You need to work on your insults, brother." Mad Dawg matched his position, feet planted securely on each side of the seat. "Lame-o."

"I'll show you lame-o." Rocker folded a hand into a fist. "Pow, right in the kisser."

"Jesus, you're in a good mood." Denver took a seat next to Rocker, leaning back on two legs. "Can't stand it when you're like this."

"You fuckin' love me and you know it." Rocker leaned closer and planted a wet kiss against Denver's cheek. "There, that should hold you over."

"Everyone loves you, man." Denver grinned at Mad Dawg around Rocker. "He's a shithead, ain't he?"

"Most days." Mad Dawg agreed, then looked towards Tinder when the man pounded the gavel against the table. "Guess we're done talkin'. Fuckin' finally."

"Okay, first piece of business is Denver's update on the HHMC. Tell us all about it, brother." Tinder sat back in his chair, angling his jaw towards the ceiling in a listening pose.

The legs of Denver's chair thumped against the floor and scraped as he pushed it back, standing. He shot Mad Dawg a glance, then looked around the room. "HHMC are no more. Well, they won't be in another week. We're killing the club and patching the few good men as Maniacs. Leadership fled south, every fuckin' one of them. Seems most of the rank and file didn't like how the club was being run and were about to revolt when one of the stupider of the fuckers got the idea of takin' Mad Dawg's Ella. We dealt with the ones directly involved, which sparked the geographic withdrawal. Me and Tinder have been over there more than we've been home, and those assholes leaving isn't a bad thing. Pullin' in the decent ones left gives us another chapter to wrangle, but they've got some good men in the mix. We've found a few we trust, and they're giving guidance on who to keep and who to cut. But"—he turned and looked at Mad Dawg with a drawn expression on his face—"that means we need to minimize those who will be in leadership positions. Since the clubhouse is situated closest to Mad Dawg, I propose we find another nomad president, and shift his rocker to a territory. Makes the most sense, but we'll need a majority agreement. Not something that can be pushed through."

"Unlike the president position before?" Mad Dawg shook his head. "You expect me to make nice with the motherfuckers who bloodied and bruised my lady?"

"No." Tinder's voice was clipped as he slapped a hand against the table. "Those assholes have been eliminated, brother. As in no longer walkin' and breathin'. We've got Ella's back, man. We do. These men didn't have a fuckin' thing to do with that action. In fact, they're as disgusted as we are by what happened. They want better for their chapter, their members. They're goddamned loyal to each other, but recognize the club wasn't loyal to them. We're only keepin' the cream of the crop. Everyone else will have to earn their patch back if they want it, but when they do they'll do it our way, not by buyin' shit."

He stared at Tinder for a breath, then sighed and dropped his chin. "I trust you, brother." He had to firm his lips against the emotion threatening to swamp him. "I apologize if my words made it sound like I didn't. I know you've got my back, every step of the way." He lifted his head and glanced around the room. "And I wanna say this out loud. I trust every one of you. I fuckin' do. Thank you, all of you, for keepin' my old lady safe. My Ella. She means… everything."

"We know." Rocker slapped his shoulder. "It's been something to watch, seein' the big, bad Mad Dawg taken down by an itty-bitty slip of a woman. Good to see, and we'll do anything needed to keep you and her on this side of goodness."

"What he said," Tinder quipped, and a ripple of chuckles moved around the room. "Now, since Mad Dawg's accepted the challenge we've put in front of him, we've got lots of logistics to work out. Next meeting, we'll do the patching and get you all acquainted. Once Dawg's got his arms wrapped around it all."

"I'll do you proud, Prez." He straightened his shoulders.

"Nothing less is acceptable," Tinder told him, and Mad Dawg nodded.

He'd do anything for his brothers and knew the same was true on their side.

Tinder slammed his palm against the table. "Second order of business is the betraying motherfucker who sold info to the HHMC assholes. He's in the wind. Denver's got a crew looking for him, but we want everyone to be aware he's outcast. Out bad, with everything that implies."

Mad Dawg's hands clenched.

In the wind.

Chapter Ten

Mad Dawg, ten months later

He gripped the handles of the heavy bags transferred to him throughout the early afternoon. Ella was walking at his side, hand tightly clasped to his forearm in excitement. They were at one of her favorite events, an author book signing in Texas.

She'd surprised him with the invitation to come with her, squealing with delight when he rapidly agreed to close down his shop for the weekend. *How could I not, when it made her so happy.*

Since then, she'd been peculiarly secretive about the weekend. Last night had been an organized dinner she'd attended alone, giving him the excuse that she'd work him hard today, so he needed his rest. An early evening meal in the hotel bar with a variety of men present had proved entertaining, as they had all been self-proclaimed book widowers. At the event with their significant others. *Just like me.*

When she'd rejoined him in the room, smiling ear to ear, he'd showed her just how little rest he really needed, loving on her so sweetly she'd wept as she came. Mad Dawg had found it wasn't uncommon for her to become overcome during lovemaking. He suspected it was because she was so in tune with her emotions, they were more easily accessed than other people. His goal every time he crawled into bed beside her was to ensure she knew she was loved. He was batting a thousand so far, because her usual response was to hover a hand over what he'd learned was the location of his heart chakra, asking him if he could feel the love.

Now, he was surrounded by hundreds of women and a few men he recognized, each of them taking turns standing in lines to pick up their preorders, or buy a book at the author's table. Often both. Every single author appeared the essence of patience, chatting as they signed books or packaged purchases, posing graciously for photos with anyone who requested it.

"We're nearly there." Ella leaned against his shoulder, resting her weight on him as she lifted to her toes. Whisper shouting into his ear, she said, "This is the table I've been waiting for!"

The author at the next table looked up and saw her, darting around and into the aisle where they stood.

"Elodie!" The recognition barely preceded the rib-cracking hug delivered by the slender woman. "I'm so glad to see you."

"You too, Sapphy. I love this event so much. It's always so much fun." Ella pulled back and gave the woman a brief kiss on her cheek. "I've got something to show you." Gripping Mad Dawg's hand, she tugged him forward a step. "Look at this. This is my boyfriend, Mad Dawg."

The woman's mouth opened, then closed as she looked up at him, then back to Ella. "Are you for real right now?"

"Uh, hi?" He wasn't certain what would be polite in response to her shocked demand. "Pleased to—"

"Jamie, get out here." She shouted as she whirled to look back and he followed with his gaze. "My husband." The banner behind her table proclaimed her Sapphire Knight, a best-selling author of a bunch of books. A man stepped out from behind the table, and this time it was Mad Dawg's turn to do a doubletake.

Jamie Knight, wearing a leather vest similar to the one Mad Dawg wore, could be his twin.

They stood there a moment, staring, then Mad Dawg set the bags at Ella's feet and stepped forwards, hand extended. Palms wrapped around wrists in a warrior's greeting, and he somehow wasn't surprised when Jamie jerked him into a one armed hug.

"Well met, brother," he murmured as they stepped apart.

"Backatcha," Jamie said with a broad grin. "Holy shit. It's like looking into a mirror. That's crazy."

"Uncanny," Sapphire agreed with a laugh as she stepped close to Jamie, leaning against him as his arm wrapped around her shoulders. "Are you two long lost brothers or something? Anything I need to know about you, hubby mine?"

"Doppelgangers," Ella said as she sidled under Mad Dawg's arm to slip her hand into his back pocket. He automatically pulled her closer. "When you put Jamie on one of your covers I had a weird moment of déjà vu, then realized it wasn't my man at all, it was your other half. Based on my discrete questioning of Dawg here, I don't think they're even related. Just doubles."

"This is so weird." Sapphire looked between the two men's faces again, then laughed. "We have got to do dinner or something. How long are you in town?"

"We leave Monday afternoon. I wanted a day to recover from all the walking." Ella laughed softly. "We don't have any plans, so whatever you want to do should work for us."

"Sounds perfect. Okay then." Sapphire clapped her hands. "Back to work for me. Elodie, do you have books? I know you've got a preorder. It's ready to go except for signatures."

"I do." Ella reached down and dug into the bag she'd brought with them.

Mad Dawg shifted his gaze from her back to Jamie, still marveling at the similarities. "You ride?" His question was met with a big smile and nod.

"Sure do. Knees in the breeze is the only way to travel." Jamie hooked a thumb over his shoulder. "I've got my duties to take care of for another two hours, then we'll tear down. The boys can help with that though. Wanna meet in the bar?"

"Absolutely." Mad Dawg dug out his phone and unlocked it, handing it over. Jamie entered a number and sent himself a text, testified to by the ding from his pants pocket. "Just let me know when you've got a minute."

Ella was standing in front of the table, chatting with Sapphire as Jamie made his way back to the author's side of the surface. Mad Dawg's gaze fixed on his woman, soaking up her pleasure and enjoyment at something so simple as connecting with an old friend.

She's absolutely the most perfect woman for me.

As if feeling the weight of his gaze on her, she glanced at him over her shoulder. Face glowing with her excitement, she blew him a kiss. He lifted a hand and caught it, then noticed another banner just up the aisle.

"Hey." He stepped closer. "Did you know D.M. Earl Is here? She's the writer with those movies we like, right?" Mad Dawg gathered the bags again, shifting the weight around until it was comfortable. "I've got Jamie's number. He'll let me know when they've got time for a drink or meal. I'm going to walk on a minute. I really want to meet D.M." He stopped short, nearly stumbling. "What do I say to her? God, am I nervous? I never got nervous even when people were shooting at me. But Tink was such a great character."

Sapphire laughed and shook her head, multicolored locks flying everywhere. "Just be yourself and tell her how much you enjoyed her work. That's all any of us ever want to hear."

"Be myself." He rolled his shoulders back, lifting his head. "Yeah. I can do that."

"Channel your inner badass," Ella told him. "You got this, Dawg."

"Oh, her name is Dawn." Jamie threw in. "She's biker, through and through. Good people. You'll do fine, man."

"Be myself, channel my badass, and remember her name is Dawn." Mad Dawg threw Ella a self-deprecating grin. "I got this."

"You so do." She lifted to her toes, lips pursed in a silent demand he was glad to meet. The kiss was gentle, closed mouthed, soft and sweet. "My badass."

"Always yours."

As he stepped around her and down the aisle, he thought fleetingly of the tiny box hidden in his drawer at her house. It was past time to let his woman know he saw them as a forever thing.

Soon as we get home and pick up Nuggie. Gonna make her my wife.

"Hi," he said to the woman in front of him as he joined the line in front of D.M.'s table.

"Hello," she responded automatically. "Wait. Holy crap. Has anyone told you how much you look like Jamie Knight?"

"Yeah," he laughed. "A couple of folks."

Her turn was next, so she faced the author and Mad Dawg glanced back to see Ella still in conversation with Sapphire. Once the woman in front of him took the perquisite selfie with the author, it was his turn.

"Hi." His mouth flapped closed and refused to open again.

"How are you?" D.M. stared up at him with a quizzical expression. "I'm D.M."

"I know. You're D.M. Earl. Dawn. You wrote Tink. My girlfriend and I love that movie. It's amazing. How you captured the actual experience of a club, even from the female perspective, is amazing. It's amazing. I already said that." Once the dam opened the stream of nonsensical words flowed without pause. "I didn't know you'd be here, or I'd have brought a book for you to sign. My girlfriend might have one, but I don't know. She's back down the way, but I couldn't wait to meet you." He sucked in a breath, willing himself to shut up. "Hi, I'm Mad Dawg."

Laughter came from beside him as Ella stepped close. "I do have a book, but I also have a preorder. Hi, D.M."

"Elodie," D.M. exclaimed, rising from her seat. "Come give me one, sister. I need me one of your good vibe hugs."

Mad Dawg stood there and watched the woman who'd become *his* favorite author hug his favorite woman, and found he was just slightly jealous.

Then D.M. stepped around the table and approached him. "Put down the bags, big man, and give me a hug."

And he did just that.

Epilogue
Elodie

Breathing in deeply, modeling what she wanted her class to do, Elodie transferred from cat/cow pose to a plank, sounding out a promise in a singsong. "We won't be here more than a count of fifteen. Just until our muscles start to tremble. Now ten, and count it down with me so I know you're breathing."

Several voices joined hers as they counted down the rest of the pose. Elodie went flat to the ground, then primed them for the next pose. "Curl your toes under and push up to your knees, then lift into downward dog. This should be as comfortable as child's pose, but if it's not, don't forget you can bend your knees, or pedal your heels to stretch out the hamstrings. This is your practice, so modify things as much as is needed for your comfort."

She was at an angle to the rest of the class and used the mirrors to review everyone's position.

From here, she also had the best view of Dom's flawless ass. Hips lifted high, he had created a perfect triangle, something she knew he'd been working on. His bare feet were flat on the mat, legs straight, and that delectable, delickable ass was on finest display in the dark leggings he'd put on for today's class.

She grinned when she caught his gaze in the mirror, nearly laughing aloud at the disgruntled expression her husband put on when he realized she'd been ogling him.

Then he smiled, and everything in her world righted, as always.

Few things made her more contented than Dominick happy.

Good vibes only.

She checked out the other students, calling out the next position, watching as Dom transitioned smoothly into the forward fold.

Off to the side, she caught sight of the coffee mug she'd finally officially confiscated from his shop. It summed up everything about her life's philosophy perfectly, and Elodie couldn't stop her giggle at the phrase.

Don't be a cuntcake.

Best. Life. Ever.

The End

THANK YOU FOR READING
Downward Dawg!

ABOUT THE COLLECTION

Motorcycles, Mobsters, and Mayhem author event proudly presents The Mayhem Makers Series.

These standalone novels are brought to you by several bestselling authors specializing in writing twisted chaos. You'll get all the bikers, mobsters, and dark romance your heart can handle.

Follow us so you never miss a new release, as they can be added in at any time!

https://amzn.to/3RKb6bL

ABOUT THE AUTHOR

Raised in the south, *Wall Street Journal* & *USA TODAY* bestselling author MariaLisa learned about the magic of books at an early age. Every summer, she would spend hours in the local library, devouring books of every genre. Self-described as a book-a-holic, she says "I've always loved to read, but then I discovered writing, and found I adored that, too. For reading...if nothing else is available, I've been known to read the back of the cereal box."

More info and extras about her books can be found on **mldemora.com**.

Want sneak peeks into what she's working on, or to chat with other readers about her books? Join the Facebook group! **bit.ly/deMora-FB-group**

deMora's got a spam-free newsletter list she'd love to have you join, too: **bit.ly/mldemora-newsletter**

~~~~~
~~~~~

ADDITIONAL SERIES AND BOOKS

Please note that books in a series frequently feature characters from additional books within that series. If series books are read out of order, readers will twig to spoilers for the other books, so going back to read the skipped titles won't have the same angsty reveals.

Rogue Maniacs MC

With a first book set within the collaborative worlds of the Mayhem Makers, these stories will introduce brand new characters and tales.

Downward Dawg, #1

Raggedy Dan, #2 (coming soon)

Tinder Heart, #3 (coming soon)

Freed Riders MC

Born from characters who simply wouldn't allow their stories to die, this spin-off series includes men and women who will be familiar to the RWMC and NTNT fans.

Gotta Dig Deep, #1

Always My Fate, #2 (coming soon)

Somewhere in Texas, #3 (coming soon)

Rebel Wayfarers MC series

A motorcycle club can be a frightening place, filled with hardened men and bad attitudes. Rebel Wayfarers is a club with their own measure of hard and dangerous, led by their national president, Davis Mason. This book series follows members as they move through their lives, filled with anguish and heartache, laughter and love. In the club, each of them find a home and family they thought long lost to them.

Mica, #1

A Sweet & Merry Christmas, #1.5

Slate, #2

Bear, #3

Jasc, #4

Gunny, #5

Mason, #6

Hoss, #7

Harddrive Holidays, #7.5

Duck, #8

Biker Chick Campout, #8.5

Watcher, #9

A Kiss to Keep You, #9.25

Gun Totin' Annie, #9.5

Secret Santa, #9.75

Bones, #10

Gunny's Pups, #10.25

Not Even A Mouse, #10.75

Fury, #11

Christmas Doings, #11.25

Gypsy's Lady includes *Never Settle* (#10.5), #11.5

Cassie, #12

Road Runner's Ride, #12.5

Occupy Yourself band series

Stardom doesn't happen overnight. Hell, it doesn't even happen after a decade in the business, as the members of Occupy Yourself have found out. But, with the right talent and the right representation, they might still have a chance to make it big. As long as they can keep their lead singer sober, keep their drummer focused on the music, keep their guitarist out of trouble … well, you get the idea. Come and join us, stand side stage for a close-up view of the backstage happenings in a rock-and-roll band. It's guaranteed to be a show you won't ever forget.

Born Into Trouble, #1

Grace In Motion, #2 (TBD)

What They Say, #3 (TBD)

Neither This, Nor That MC series

Legends are born from moments like these. Folktales spun around a single point in time so perfect, you can almost hear the click resonating through the universe as things align. Meet Twisted, Po'Boy, Retro, and Ragman, good old boys from southern states who have many things in common. First, is a bone-deep love of the biker lifestyle. Second, would be their love of the brotherhood, and knowing that you trust the man at your back. Finally, these men have the love of a good woman. None of these come without a price, and it is our pleasure to journey along with them as they discover the blessings that can be won, and lost along the way.

This Is the Route Of Twisted Pain, #1

Treading the Traitor's Path: Out Bad, #2

Shelter My Heart, #3

Trapped by Fate on Reckless Roads, #4

Tarnished Lies and Dead Ends, #5

Tangled Threats on the Nomad Highway, #6

Rebel Wayfarers crossover stories

Enjoy these stories that tie the different worlds of my MC universe together, bringing Rebel Wayfarers MC and clubs like Neither This Nor That and other series into glorious alignment.

Going Down Easy

No Man's Land

In Search of Solace

Mayhan Bucklers MC series

The Mayhan Bucklers MC has been part of the rolling hills of Northeast Texas for decades. Now, new life is being breathed into this reborn club, a legacy resurrected by grandsons of the founder. The MBMC is set to surpass its original glory, fortified with an honorable purpose: Helping wounded warriors reintegrate back into society, gifting those who've given so much with a safe place to land.

Learning how to navigate life while war still echoes inside you isn't easy, but with solid brothers at your back, anything is possible.

Most Rikki-Tik, #1

Mad Minute, #2

Pucker Factor, #3

Boocoo Dinky Dau, #4

Borderline Freaks MC series

When you can't count on anyone else to save you, there's only one real choice. Borderline Freaks MC is a series of books about the men of the club and their brotherhood — and of course the love they have for their women. Take a trip along with Monk, Blade, Wolf, and Neptune, and feel for yourself the connection these men have for each other.

Service and Sacrifice, #1

More Than Enough, #2

Lack of In-between, #3

See You in Valhalla, #4

Alace Sweets series

Dark romantic thrillers, these books are not light reads. Filled with edge-of-your-seat suspense, these intense stories command the reader's attention as they drive towards their explosive endings. Alace Sweets is a vigilante serial killer, with everything that implies and is sure to trip all your triggers. Be ready.

Alace Sweets, #1

Seeking Worthy Pursuits, #2

Embarrassment of Monsters, #3

All the Broken Rules, #4 (TBD)

With My Whole Heart series

Sweet as pie and twice as delicious, these romantic love stories are a guaranteed happily-ever-after read.

With My Whole Heart, #1

Bet On Us, #2

**If You Could Change One Thing:
Tangled Fates Stories**

When threads in the tapestry of life are cut short, inexorably changing the future for those you love, would you be willing to tempt fate to set things right?

There Are Limits, #1

Rules Are Rules, #2

The Gray Zone, #3

Additional Books:

Hard Focus

Dirty Bitches MC: Season 3

~~~~~
~~~~~

deMora's Rebel Wayfarers MC and the Neither This Nor That MC series do intertwine, along with the Occupy Yourself band books, so readers have a couple of choices. Each series can be read independently beginning with RWMC, OYBS, and then NTNT without too many spoilers. There's also a merger between deMora's RWMC world and Lila Rose's Hawks MC world. Or they can be read intertwined—in chronological order.

See below for the recommended reading order if you want to follow according to timing:

Mica, RWMC #1

A Sweet & Merry Christmas, RWMC #1.5

Slate, RWMC #2

Bear, RWMC #3

Born Into Trouble, OYBS #1

Jase, RWMC #4

Gunny, RWMC #5

Mason, RWMC #6

Hoss, RWMC #7

This Is the Route of Twisted Pain, NTNT #1

Harddrive Holidays, RWMC #7.5

Duck, RWMC #8

Biker Chick Campout, RWMC #8.5

Watcher, RWMC #9

Treading the Traitor's Path: Out Bad, NTNT #2

Living Without, Lila Rose's Hawks MC: Caroline Springs #4

Shelter My Heart, NTNT #3

A Kiss to Keep You, RWMC #9.25

Gun Totin' Annie, RWMC #9.5

Secret Santa, RWMC #9.75

Trapped by Fate on Reckless Roads, NTNT #4

Bones, RWMC #10

Gunny's Pups, RWMC #10.25

Not Even A Mouse, RWMC #10.75

Road Runner's Ride, RWMC #12.5

Never Settle, RWMC #10.5

Fury, RWMC #11

Christmas Doings, RWMC #11.25

Gypsy's Lady, RWMC #11.5

Tarnished Lies and Dead Ends, NTNT #5

Going Down Easy

No Man's Land

In Search of Solace

Tangled Threats on the Nomad Highway, NTNT #6

Cassie, RWMC #12

More information available at **mldemora.com**.

www.ingramcontent.com/pod-product-compliance
Lightning Source LLC
Chambersburg PA
CBHW061304210726
48293CB00003B/1105